NICK GRAINGER

THE SEARCH FOR ATLANTIS

BOOK TWO

G.W. Mullins

Light Of The Moon Publishing

ISBN: 978-1-958221-25-9

First Printing

This is a work of fiction. Names, characters, businesses, places, events, and incidents are either the products of the author's imagination or used in a fictitious manner. Any resemblance to actual persons, living or dead, or actual events is purely coincidental.

Light Of The Moon Publishing has allowed this work to remain exactly as the author intended, verbatim, without editorial input.

Printed in the United States of America

For books available from G.W. Mullins in
Hardback, Paperback and eBook

Visit: https://gwmullins.wixsite.com/books

Or scan the QR Code below

Links to G.W. Mullins pages are on Linktree
https://linktr.ee/gw.mullins

What begins as a simple, bittersweet tale about a man turned into a polar bear, grandly unfolds into a rich, mythical adventure, in this best-selling book series.

Based on Hans Christian Andersen's fairy tale, author G.W. Mullins expands on this classic story creating a new mythology that takes readers into the land of snow and ice.

G.W. Mullins

Rise Of The Snow Queen
Book Series

The Polar Bear King

War Of The Witches

The Story of Gerda and Kai

Rise Of The Snow Queen Series

What begins as a simple, bittersweet tale about a man turned into a polar bear, grandly unfolds into a rich, mythical adventure in this best-selling book series.

Based on Hans Christian Andersen's fairy tale, author G.W. Mullins expands on this story creating a new mythology that takes readers into the world of snow and ice.

Long before the adventures of Gerda and Kai, this story takes readers to a remote mountain village, where Winter claims lives, at the Snow Queen's command. The story goes back to the Mirror and how it cracked, sending its shards into the world to infect the innocent.

This reimagining embarks on a much more adult tone with the mood turning rather sinister, as the Snow Queen battles to obtain the mirror. The story will capture and pull you in as Gerda and Kai make their appearances by the third book in the series.

Rise Of The Snow Queen Series

Book One: The Polar Bear King
Book Two: The War Of The Witches
Book Three: The Story Of Gerda And Kai

From
The
Dead
Of
Night
Book Series
Death is only the beginning.
Daniel walked in the land of the Dead.
Now the Dead want him back
Daniel Is Waiting
Daniel Returns
Daniel Awakens
Daniel's Fate
G.W. Mullins

From the Dead Of Night Series

Death Is Only The Beginning. Daniel walked into the land of the dead. Now the dead want him back!

Daniel Stratton died in a tragic accident. His life should have been over, but it was not. His spirit spent the next sixty years trying to communicate with the people who came to the cemetery. Then, Jen came one night to the mausoleum, seeking refuge from a life that was spinning out of control. It was there she found Daniel.

As they work to free him from the cemetery; they learn that the Light comes for all dead, Daniel is forced to enter it. Inside he sees seven Shadow People within the light, and each one marks him. Daniel knows these Shadows will come for him. Each one in the body of a human who has just died. To survive, Daniel and Jen must escape the "Shadows" that are coming for them.

From the Dead Of Night Series

Book One: Daniel Is Waiting
Book Two: Daniel Returns
Book Three Daniel Awakens
Book Four: Daniel's Fate

Best-Selling Author G.W. Mullins speaks to the
dead and talks about
After Death Communication in his book series...
Messages
From The
Other Side
Stories of the Dead, Their Communication, and Unfinished Business
Messages From The Other Side
Crossing Over
Available in Hardback, Paperback and eBook

Messages From The Other Side Series

Best-selling author G.W. Mullins shares his personal journey toward understanding death, the afterlife, and communication with the spirits of loved ones who have passed over. In "Messages From The Other Side Stories of the Dead, Their Communication, and Unfinished Business," Mullins tells of dealing with the grief of his mother's passing and the reassurance of an after-death communication that changed his outlook towards death and grief.

This book not only tells of Mullins' personal journey into understanding but also guides others to understand why we receive communications and the signs to look for. Mullins also explores visitation dreams and tells of his own experience in the area and shares the stories of others who have had similar experiences.

This book highlights the author's journey in an exploration for knowledge, and his understanding that, without question, there is life after death.

Messages From The Other Side Series

**Book One: Messages From The Other Side
Book Two: Crossing Over**

In order to save his uncle, Malachi is forced to summon
Santa Muerte, the deity of death. With his soul on the
line, he must do her bidding, to regain his freedom.

To fight evil, you have to
embrace the darkness

Rise
Of The
DarkLighter

From Best-Selling Author

G.W.
Mullins

Dark Awakening
Night Of The Demon
Available in Hardback, Paperback and eBook

Rise Of The Dark Lighter Series

Mullins returns to the familiar world he created for the "From The Dead Of Night" series while building a new story in this universe. In the book "Daniel's Fate," Mullins left his audience with an ending that promised more. In this latest book, he delivers, with a continuation of the final battle between good and evil.

To save his uncle, Malachi is forced to summon Santa Muerte, the deity of death. He offers a year of his life in exchange for her help. With his soul on the line, he must do her bidding, to regain his freedom.

The dead begin to rise, as Angels and Demons prepare to wage war for control of humanity. Malachi must choose a side as Armageddon begins.

"Dark Awakening" is the first of three books from "Rise Of The Dark Lighter." This new series is a continuation of his "From The Dead Of Night" books.

Rise Of The DarkLighter

Book One: Dark Awakening
Book Two: Night Of The Demon

Danni liked the quiet upstate New York house she had moved to...
Until she realized something else was living in the house with her.

VENGEANCE

G.W. Mullins

SOMETIMES
THE THINGS YOU CANNOT SEE,
CAN BE THE MOST DEADLY.

G.W. Mullins

Available worldwide in Hardback, Paperback and eBook

Vengeance
A Paranormal Murder Mystery

"Mystery, Murder, Paranormal Events, and a story that leaves you guessing as the bodies stack up."
– Matthew Trent OutLoud Magazine

After the death of her father, Danni starts a new life in a seaside town in New York where she and her mother move into a strange Gothic house with a terrible history. From the moment Danni gets there, she feels she is being watched. She is sure they are not alone in the house.

As Danni learns of her new home, she is told of a past resident who fell to her death on the nearby cliffs at the same time that her teenage daughter, Elizabeth, disappeared.

Elizabeth's spirit appears to Danni and claims that her mother's death was a murder, not suicide, and asks for Danni's help in bringing the dangerous killer to justice.

The mystery unfolds as Danni enlists the help of the hunky new friend she has made named Joe. A romance develops between them, but does Joe know more about the murder and disappearance than he is letting on? Will Danni live to solve the murder?

As the city darkens and humans descend into sleep, a powerful entity known as the Sand Man, takes control of our dreams and nightmares.
DREAM WALKER
Don't Fall Asleep,
The SandMan Is Coming!
Enter The SandMan
Wide Awake In Dreamland
Available in Hardback, Paperback and eBook
G.W. Mullins

Dream Walker Series

They say a dream is a wish, but what they forgot to mention, nightmares are dreams too. As the city darkens and humans descend into sleep, a powerful being enters the Earth Realm. This mysterious creature, known as the Sandman, takes control of our dreams and battles for control of our souls.

After a boy named Zach is taken into the other realm, he awakens to a new world filled with nightmares. He is joined by two others, Daniel and Jen, as they battle to escape the Dream World and find their way back to reality. Beware the Sandman is coming.

"Enter The Sandman" is the first of three books from Author G.W. Mullins' "Dream Walker" book series. This new series shares a couple of familiar faces from the Best-Selling "From The Dead Of Night" books, featuring the Best-Selling titles "Daniel Is Waiting" and "Daniel Returns."

Dream Walker Series

Book One: Enter The SandMan
Book Two: Wide Awake In Dreamland

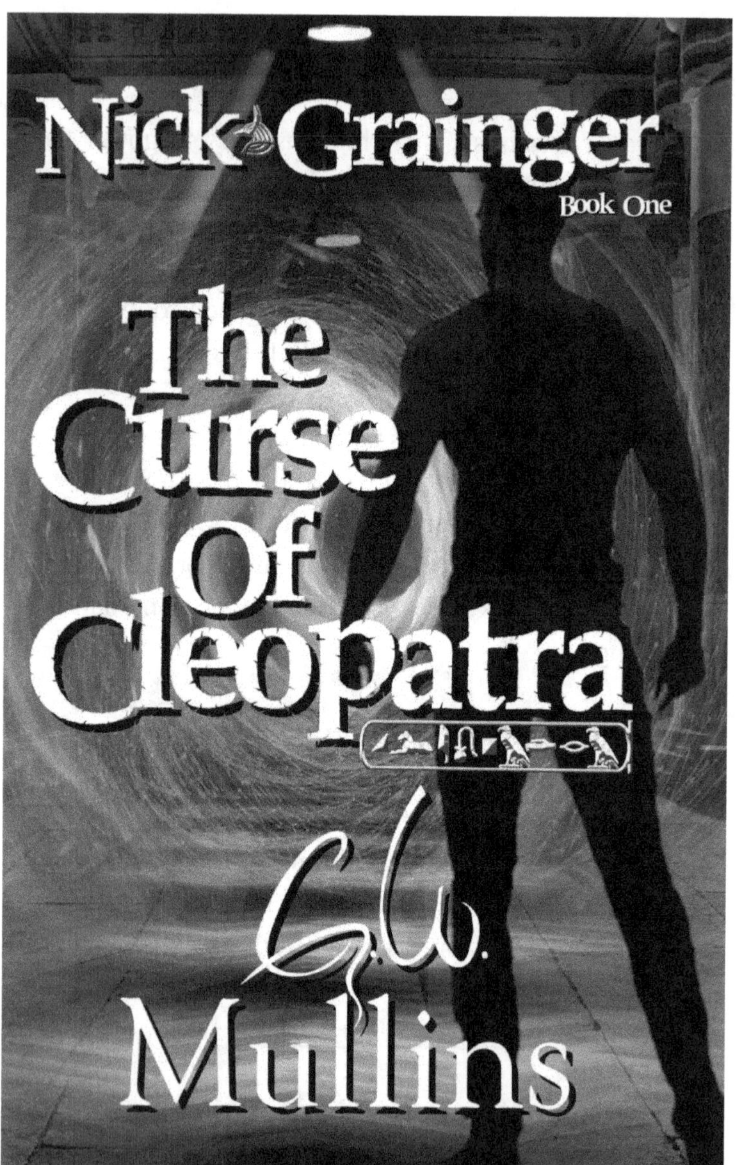
Nick Grainger
Book One
The Curse Of Cleopatra
G.W. Mullins

Nick Grainger Series

Building on the concept that the Earth was once populated by a superior Ancient Alien race, this new book series takes the reader on an adventure through gateways to the multiverse.

Nick Grainger, a young college student working on an archaeological dig in Egypt, accidentally activates a gate to a different universe. He along with three of his companions, are thrown into the ancient alien gateway system between parallel worlds. Lost in the multiverse, they must search for a way home.

On their journey, their gate opens into strange new worlds, similar to their Earth, but in different times and in places. It is on one such Earth, they arrive in Egypt, not as it was in the days of the ancients. Now, it is a place where a technologically advanced race of gods rule.

These new gods of Egypt live through taking the bodies of human hosts. It is there, that Nick must fight his ultimate battle, as he is designated to be host to the god Anubis.

"Nick Grainger The Curse Of Cleopatra" is the first of three books from Author G.W. Mullins' "Nick Grainger" book series.

FROM THE AUTHOR OF "RISE OF THE SNOW QUEEN - THE POLAR BEAR KING" AND "DANIEL IS WAITING"

THE LEGEND OF WHITE BEAR

Extended Edition

EVERYONE HAS A BEAST WITHIN THEM...

G.W. MULLINS

The Legend Of White Bear (Extended Edition)

Nita's tribe faced the coming of the bear every full moon. When it came, many would die.

To protect his daughter, the chief sent her away to live in a rip in time and space, called the void. He told her it was for her protection, but he never told her of the bear's history.

One member of his tribe was burdened with carrying the bear shapeshifter trait. For a lifetime, they would be cursed with being both human and bear until their death. Then a new child would be born to carry the trait.

While in the void, Nita discovers the true horrifying history of the white bear.

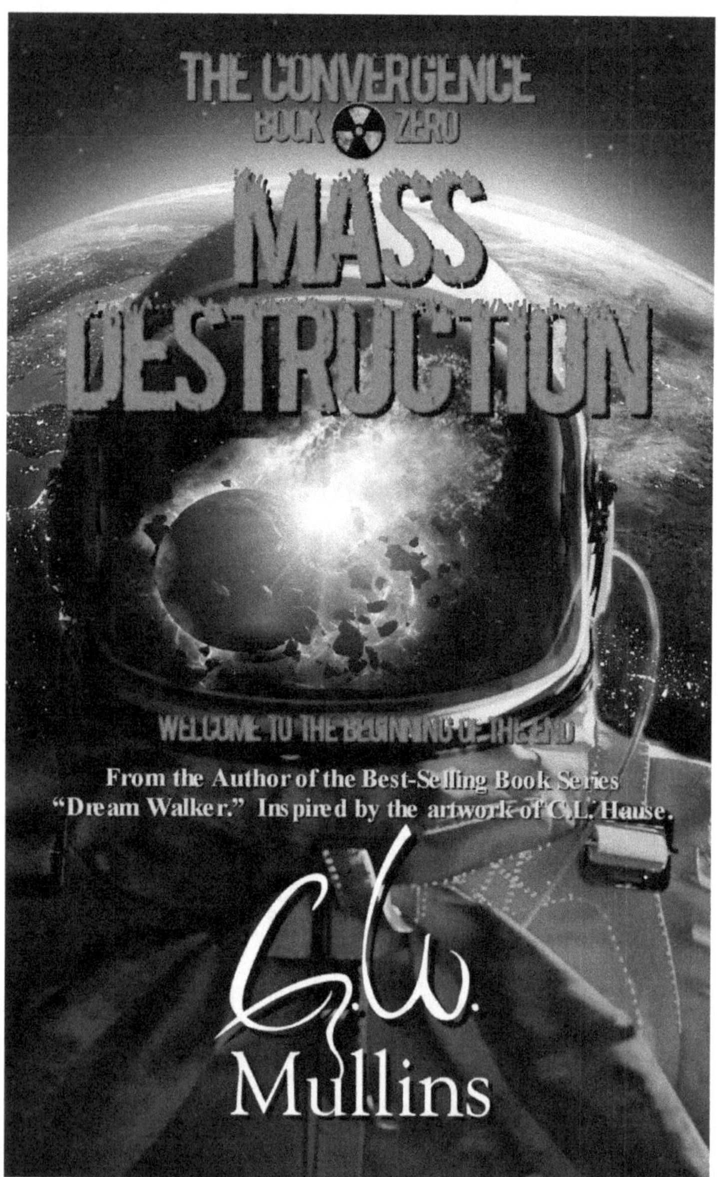
THE CONVERGENCE
BOOK ZERO
MASS
DESTRUCTION
WELCOME TO THE BEGINNING OF THE END
From the Author of the Best-Selling Book Series
"Dream Walker." Inspired by the artwork of C.L. Hause.
G.W.
Mullins

The Convergence Series

In the year 2029, the third world war will begin. After the global population is pushed to the brink of insanity from the recent pandemic, they plunge into hatred and violence. With the space race to colonize the moon, man seeks a refuge from the insanity, and the impending environmental destruction brought on by decades of pollution.

In the worldwide confusion, the inevitable happens, when a single nuclear warhead is fired by the command of an insane dictator. Nuclear retaliations are sent forward, ending in the destruction of the Earth's moon. The end of mankind as we know will begin. Human civilization is cast in ruin. A strange new world rises from the old; a world of mutation, super science, and magic. Witness the Convergence. The countdown begins now.

The Convergence Series

Book Zero: Mass Destruction
Book One: Armageddon

Other titles available from G.W. Mullins include:

Night Of The Walkers

Timeless - An Adult Paranormal Romance Novel

Aliens, Gods, And Other Paranormal Native American Tales

The Native American Story Book Volume 1-5- Stories Of The American Indians For Children

Walking With Spirits Volumes 1-6 Native American Myths, Legends, And Folklore

The Native American Cookbook

Star People, Sky Gods, And Other Tales of The Native American Indians

More Star People, Sky Gods, and Other Paranormal Tales Of The Native American Indians

Included at the end of this book, are the first chapters of G.W. Mullins' Best-Selling Series "The Convergence" Book Zero "Mass Destruction"

For Clarence

"Anubis was considered to be the god of death himself, who had the power to resurrect a soul, if called upon. But the resurrection came at a price Something had to be offered in return."

"But afterwards there occurred violent earthquakes and floods; and in a single day and night of misfortune all your warlike men in a body sank into the earth, and the island of Atlantis in like manner disappeared in the depths of the sea."
— **Plato, Timaeus and Critias**

An excerpt from
Nick Grainger Book One
The Curse Of Cleopatra

Chapter Twenty-One:
Challenge of the Gods

From the ships floating above, the Replicants began appearing on the ground, out of beams of light. As they walked forward, Thoth studied them. Cocking his head sideways, he was amused by their design.

"Yes, human, but not human. Part machine, but not whole machine. They have implanted mechanical parts in their bodies. This is fascinating. How could they live like that?" Thoth was excited at the concept.

"You built mini computers to revive the gods. It's really not that different." Emma jabbed at him.

"No, this is very different. They are absorbing other cultures and people into their own. I have never seen such a dangerous race in person."

"Uhh, about that." Nick looked hard at him.

"Yes, I am aware, I have no body. I am still a living being in hologram form."

"Well, that is good for you, they won't be able to take you." The Professor shook his head.

"Perhaps they could. If they are seeking technology, they could always find my main computer." Thoth looked scared as he transported himself back to his chamber.

In front of him, two Replicants stood studying his mechanical form. As he approached, they did not acknowledge him. They were not there for conversation; it was his advanced computer system they wanted.

As the one reached in to remove a part of his processor, Thoth split into multiples of himself and attacked. For a brief amount of time, he solidified his form and had form. His victory was a short-lived one, as new Replicants appeared to take the place of those who he destroyed.

Thoth erected a shield around his processor and headed back to the city square where he found the others still watching the children of the gods, being rounded up and frozen in place to be absorbed.

Thoth called out mentally to the gods. One by one they assembled. Around them, their children stood frozen. They attacked in unison, knocking the Replicant's ships from the sky.

Ra came forward, he was growing weary of the creatures. Holding his arms out wide, he called upon the sun as he turned his power against their enemies. His power was great, the Replicants were unyielding.

Nick walked forward, as the others watched. He looked around at the enemy and studied them. As he blinked his eyes, a familiar blue light returned. A data stream filled his vision as he looked for a weakness.

Nick turned loose the power he had been hiding since Anubis occupied his body. As his whole body began to glow, he aimed his light at the invaders one by one. His voice projected outwards as he locked onto each Replicant.

"I see your heart is heavy in your time of death. I will help you deal with your pain, as I cross you over to the afterlife. I will guide you."

As Nick's body began to spin around, he was lifted into the air as he sought out the lives he chose to escort into the afterlife. His reach covered the whole city. As the Replicants tried to flee, he claimed many of their invasion fleet.

Drifting back to the sand, Nick fell onto his side. Thoth moved in his direction, as he studied Nick to see if he was still alive. A groan came from deep inside Nick as Thoth shook his head.

"He is alive and still very much himself."

"How did he do that without the mask." The Professor asked.

"I am not one to admit ignorance. But in this case, I do not know. Perhaps there was still some lingering energy trapped within.

"Let's hope that was all it was," Emma said as she pulled Nick's head into her lap.

She looked down at his face, as he opened his eyes. There was no blue glow. He looked up to her and smiled. His body was exhausted, but his mind was free.

"Can we go home already?" He asked trying to raise his head.

"Rest, you have earned it. I will have you moved back to my chamber, where you and your friends will be safe until I locate your gate coordinates." Thoth said as multiple versions of himself arrived to take Nick away and care for the wounded children of the gods.

"I see why Inak was so scared of the Replicants. His people did not have gods to defend them." The Professor commented.

"I am scared Professor," Shabakaa added.

"Why, I would think you were feeling good to have survived all you have been through in the last few days."

"I do feel fortunate, but if the Replicants can come here and do what they tried to do. Who is to say they cannot go elsewhere in the multiverse? What if they find their way to our Earth?"

"Sadly, they could, and they could do damage. But, if we make it home, we will be there to warn our people. We have an advantage now, we have knowledge." The Professor said smiling.

"I guess you're right. Now, we just have to find our way home." Shabakaa pushed down his fears. For now, all he wanted was to see his family and friends again. He was willing to put his faith in Thoth's abilities.

An excerpt from
Nick Grainger Book One
The Curse Of Cleopatra

Chapter Twenty-Two:
Gateway to Home

"Your journey is done now. It is time for you to go home. You have earned that much." Thoth spoke as he led the travelers to the obelisk.

"I never thought a gateway could look so good." The Professor replied.

Emma trailed behind with Nick, as the others reached the gate. She stopped and took his hand. She smiled as he turned to look her in the face. He felt more like himself, there was no longer a struggle to keep Anubis at bay.

"I am glad I got to know more of you during this adventure," Emma said as she held tight to him.

"Oh, so we are calling this an adventure?" He laughed, almost choking on the words.

"Yeah, I think adventure is so much nicer than what really happened."

"You know, when we step back through the gate and go back home, nothing will ever be the same again," Nick said looking out across the sand.

"Do we tell people?"

"No way. Besides, who would believe us?"

As they caught up with the group, Thoth turned to look at them. He was never one for attachments, but these people, he liked. He felt a kind of sadness to see them leave. He was sure he would never see them again.

"Today, you have Thoth's respect. You have taught me much, with my vast array of experience and wisdom, that is saying something. I look forward to remembering you."

"We'll remember you too. It's not every day you meet a hologram of a god from ancient Egypt." Shabakaa said laughing.

"You found our way home?" Emma asked.

"Yes, it took some time and research of the gate system. I did find your planet, which was not easy, being there were discrepancies in the records. It is all set to go. Nick, you just have to use your red crystal and activate it."

Nick moved to the edge of the table and pulled the crystal from his pocket. Placing it on the table, the other crystals all began to glow. As the group moved back a few steps, the wormhole began to form.

As Nick and the others said goodbye, they moved towards the opening one by one. Thoth looked on as the travelers walked through the gate and they disappeared into the swirl of bright color. And then, they were gone and Thoth turned away.

In an ice-covered cave a few minutes later an obelisk much like the one they came through began to light up and then formed the end of a wormhole. As the travelers came flying through and landed on the ground, Nick stood up and looked around.

"Where the hell are we?" He asked as if he would get an answer.

"It appears, Thoth made a mistake." The Professor replied.

"I don't understand, he said he found our planet. This is not the tomb we left from." Emma said as she shivered from the cold.

"It must be in the minus numbers here. We will freeze to death." Shabakaa shook as he tried to get the words out.

"I agree. I am going to look out the front of the cave, but if I see nothing in sight, we will have to leave or we will freeze to death."

Nick looked out into the snow squall that beat against the opening of the cave. The freezing blasts hurt his eyes and stung his face. They had no choice; they had to leave and fast.

Returning to the others, he held up the crystal and shook his head. He hoped they would do better on their next gate. Nick's hand shook as he put the crystal into place. He had a numbness starting in his fingers.

As the gate lit up and the familiar wormhole formed in front of them, for once it was a welcome sight. They wasted no time going through the gate. As their forms disappeared, the gate powered down and went into its dormant state.

Minutes later, outside the cave, the roar of a jet plane flew past. Coming in closer, it flew circles around the location. "This is Arctic Echo 1542; I located an energy source in the area of Mt. Gunnbjörn. It just appeared and disappeared a few minutes later. I don't know how to explain it. This storm is getting pretty bad, I will have to return to base. When the weather breaks, we will be able to investigate this further. If there was life here, it is gone now."

Before

"Can anyone hear me?" Emma screamed out as she swung her arms and legs to stay above the water.

"I'm here," Nick called back to her. "I just don't know, where here is."

"Why is it so dark here? I can't see anything." Emma said back to him.

"I don't know, it is as if there is no sun." He said as he swam in the direction of her voice. "Keep talking, I will find you."

"Where are the others? I don't hear any other voices." She said, feeling the chill of the water creep through her body.

"I don't know. I only heard you, and then, not for a while after we arrived here."

"They did come through the gate with us…didn't they?" Fear filled her, at the thought that their friends had been lost.

"Yes, I saw them in the wormhole, just ahead of me. I just don't know where they could be." Nick spoke his last word, as he floated into Emma.

Turning towards him, Emma threw her arms around Nick's neck. She was reassured by his presence. Nick looked out into the darkness, barely able to see her face. He didn't want to scare her, but there was little hope in him finding their friends.

"Nick, if we are here, then where is the gate we came through?"

"I have no idea. I remember the wormhole opening as we reached this address. I just don't remember much past the point of being thrown out. The others have to be here, but the gate can't be above us."

"Then it has to be below. Nick, could it be under the water?" Emma tried to rationalize how this could be.

"If it is below us, then we were ejected into the depths of whatever this is. I hope this water is not too deep. If it is, I don't know how we will get the gate activated, and go through it."

"It is simple, you hold your breath." A voice came from behind them.

"Shabakaa, you made it! I was so scared something had happened to you." Emma yelled out.

"No, I am very much alive. Just not enjoying the darkness." He replied. Where is the Professor?"

"We don't know. We just found each other minutes ago." Nick said as he fumbled to get his hand in his pocket. "Maybe I have a solution for the moment."

As Nick tugged at the object in his pocket, he freed it and raised his hand out of the water. Twisting the end of the shaft, a light-filled the area.

As they raised their heads, the three began to wish they still did not know where they were.

"Nick, what are those?" Emma bravely raised her voice.

"I would say some kind of warships, and they do not look friendly," Nick said as he grabbed tight to Emma's arm.

"Do you think anyone is on board?" Shabakaa asked.

"Yes, most certainly, and if you want to live, put out that light, before they find us." The Professor called out, trying to tread the water,

Nick put out the light, as they all gathered together. "Professor, where have you been? We thought you were dead."

"No, my boy, not dead just yet. When I came out of the wormhole, I swam into the side of one of the ships. I made my way onboard and saw them. I have never been so scared in my life." The Professor tried to catch his breath. "Nick, we have to get to the gate and get out of here. These beings are slavers. They collect species, to use them for hard labor. If they capture us, we will never escape."

"I understand, but to escape, we need a gateway. Where is it?" Nick insisted.

"It is below us, under the water. The good news is, it is not all that far down to it. We should be able to hold our breath, long enough to get to it." The Professor tried to be reassuring.

"And the bad news?" Emma said sarcastically.

"There is no light here. We have to get to this gate in the darkness of the water, and then activate it."

"You have to be kidding," Shabakaa said as he punched his hand into the water.

"No, wait, there might be a way. I have the light. If we get down far enough, they might not be able to see it, or us. I mean, what choice do we have? Die in the water, or by their hands." Nick did not want to die either way, but trying to get to another gate sounded better than slavery.

"Ok, agreed. Everyone, take a deep breath and swim quickly straight down. I will turn on the light as we descend. Just follow the light, and pray we find the gate."

As the four made their way down into the water, Nick turned on the light and they converged on each other. Aiming the light down, he saw the shape of a stone doorway. It was the gate. The pressure of the water surrounded them, as they touched down in front of it.

Nick pulled the red crystal from his pocket, as he wiped the surface of the dialer. It was intact. As he tried to activate the power, he heard a sound from behind. A ray of light illuminated the area around the four of them.

Turning, Nick saw the lifeform, as much alien as humanoid. He turned back to his task, as the force of a second blast flew past his head. He was not willing to give up after they had come so far. He would rather die in the water than be taken.

As the blasts came faster, he looked down at the

controller. There was power.

Chapter One: Escape to Freedom

The light of the blasts was like the first light of morning, under the water. It made Nick's job a little easier. As he used the red crystal, the device dialed. He didn't know where they were going, but he hoped it was better than where they were leaving. He did not have time to devise an escape route. He had little time left before the oxygen in his system was completely depleted.

The device lit up, as the familiar swirl of light circled inside, and then projected outwards. The others converged on the gate as Nick turned towards the creatures, that had gathered behind them. He motioned for the others to enter the gate as he looked upon their would-be captors.

The Professor and Emma were first through into the wormhole, then as Shabakaa prepared to enter, he looked back to Nick. Something felt wrong or out of place. He watched closely as Nick faced the enemy.

Nick raised his hands, and a blast of energy flew forward, disintegrating everything in its path. Shabakaa just floated there for a moment, watching in disbelief. He saw Nick begin to move, as he jumped into the gateway.

As Nick moved forward, passing through the water, his eyes still glowed with a brilliant blue light. A grin covered his face, as he made his way to the opening. In the wormhole, the blue light faded, and Nick once again became normal. He had no memory of the destruction he just caused or much past the dialing of the gate.

Shabakaa flew through the network, still stunned by what he witnessed. He was sure he knew how it had occurred, but it should not have been possible. Nick was cleansed of Anubis. There should have been no way for the life force to possess him. No matter what, he knew he had to pay attention to future events, and when the time was right, he would tell the others.

At the end of the wormhole, they all flew forward with a wave of water, that had followed them through the gateway. Slamming to the ground, the water washed over them once again. Emma let out a scream, she had been through too much. The last wave of water was just like an insult.

"Damn!" Emma had no trouble showing her displeasure in the situation.

"Calm down sweetheart. There are people in the desert, that would appreciate this much water. Maybe even less." Shabakaa said laughing.

Emma raised herself up to meet him, eye to eye. "No one, and I mean no one, calls me sweetheart. So back off, before I rip you a new one."

"Calm down Emma, he was only joking." Nick tried to separate them. "You were only joking, right?" Nick said smiling.

"Um, yes, I think," Shabakaa said swallowing hard.

"I would check your sense of humor in bad times. It doesn't flow well." The Professor added.

"Yeah, and next time, I might not stop her from killing you." Nick tried to contain his laughter.

"So, where the hell are we now?" Emma asked as she stood up, and let the water drip from her clothes.

"If I did not know better, I would say, New York," Nick said studying the landscape.

"How do you know?" The Professor asked scanning for any familiar landmarks.

"I know because my parents used to live near here. Just a couple of miles down this road." Happiness filled Nick as he stood up and pointed the way. "I know we are not home, but this is definitely better than the black hole of water we just left."

"Yeah, about that, we really need to be able to control where we are traveling. We went from freezing to death, to almost drowning. Then possible enslavement. I for one am over it." Emma spouted out her dissatisfaction, as they began to walk.

"Yes, I also have a problem with a life as someone's slave." Shabakaa laughed out loud.

"Ditto." The Professor added.

"Hey guys, I got us out of there. We are still alive. We lived to fight another day." Nick just stood smiling at them. "No alien slaves here.

They all walked down the road, trying to ignore the discomfort from their wet clothes. No one was in the mood for humor, yet they all knew they were lucky. Still, Shabakaa watched Nick carefully. He was fearful of Anubis, and the possibility there was still a hold over Nick. For now, there was nothing he could do about it.

They walked for over five miles until they reached city streets, lined with houses. Their clothes had dried, but the feeling of disgust still filled each one of them. Emma dragged her feet filled with exhaustion. Her body was reaching its breaking point.

"How much further do we have to go? I can't take much more of this today." Emma moaned.

"We don't have to go any further," Nick said quietly.

"Why, is this not the right place?" Shabakaa asked.

"No, it is the right place. That is the house." He said as he pointed in front of them. "That is my parent's house.

As they approached the door, it swung open, and an older woman in a dress and apron stepped forward. Nick studied her face. He tried to open his mouth, but no words came out. The only thing he could do was manage the lump in his throat.

"Hello darling, you are home early. I see you brought friends from the university. Don't be rude, introduce me to them."

Nick went through the formalities and everyone was welcomed into the house. Nick tried to act normally but did not have the strength to face what was before him.

"Why is Nick acting so weird?" Emma whispered back to the others, as they followed her.

"Because my dear, Nick's mother on our earth, died five years ago. It would seem, things are different here. I wonder where his father is." The Professor was uneasy about discussing the situation.

"What was that Professor?" Mrs. Grainger asked.

"Oh, it was not important." He responded.

"Don't be embarrassed to ask. My husband died five years ago in a car crash. I am not as sensitive about it these days." She said trying to smile.

As she left the room, Nick turned to the others. "It is flipped. This multiverse never ceases to amaze me. It seems like there can be so many similarities to our own world, but there is always that one change."

"What do we do?" Shabakaa asked.

"We eat, get cleaned up, and then we continue on our journey. I mean, what choice do we have, our friends, family, and loved ones are on a different earth." Nick insisted.

"And what do we do when the alternate version of you, shows up tonight for dinner?" Emma asked.

"I have no idea."

Chapter Two: The Man from the Future

The evening wore on like a forced family reunion. Nick tried to interact with the woman, who in every way, was his mother. She was slightly older, but she would have been on his earth if she did not die. In his mind, he searched for one thing, anything that was different. He could not find it. Nothing was out of place. Nothing made him question her existence.

As dinner came and went, Emma grew restless. She knew they had to get out of the house before the Nick from this planet showed up. She glanced at Nick from time to time and tried to get his attention. He was in such a state of shock, that he did not even notice her.

Pulling Shabakaa aside, Emma tried to not be heard by Mrs. Grainger. "We are running out of time. If the other Nick shows up, we are going to have a lot of explaining to do. I really do not want to be a part of that." Emma's rant ended as her air ran out.

"I agree. I have already spoken with the Professor. We need to leave now. We have been here two hours and that is too long. We are clean, and have been fed. There is no reason to stay here." Shabakaa whispered. "We need to corner Nick, and get him to leave."

Shabakaa moved closer to Nick and moved a hand to the back of his shoulder. "We need to talk for a moment."

"About?" Nick said smiling at his mother.

"We have an errand to run. If the four of us do not get going, we will miss out on the opportunity." Shabakaa said trying to be polite.

"Were you supposed to be somewhere Nick? Don't let me hold you up if you and your friends have an appointment." Mrs. Grainger said with a smile on her face.

"Yeah, I guess we have to go. I just wish I could stay longer."

"It's OK, you will be home soon, I am sure." Mrs. Grainger said as she pulled him into a hug.

"Goodbye, Mom." Was all Nick could say, as he pulled away and turned for the door.

"Nice to have met you all. Have a wonderful night." She said waving to them, as they walked down the cement driveway.

Nick didn't look back. It was too hard. He was just beginning to accept her as being alive. She wasn't his real mom, but in a way…she was. In his mind, he tried to be rational. He knew, that nothing they encountered on these earths, was his own. He just walked faster, as the group tried to keep up.

"Nick, you need to slow down a little. I know you are upset, but we don't even know where we are going." Emma called out.

Then, he stopped in his tracks. Emma was right. They had to locate the gateway, and then figure out where to go next. He turned to face them as a sad look crossed his face. "She could have been my mother, you know. If she had lived." Nick's voice trailed off as Emma put her arms around him, and pulled his head to her shoulder.

No one spoke for a moment. No one knew what to say. The Professor lowered his eyes to the ground. He felt bad for Nick but didn't know how anyone could help this situation. Shabakaa wanted to feel bad about everything, but his mind raced back to the glowing eyes of Anubis. He knew the truth, but this was not the time.

As Emma released Nick, he moved back and smiled at her. "Thank you, that helped more than you will ever know."

"Good, that gets us a little more back on course. Now, where do we go from here?"

No one saw the man emerge from the tree line. He was quiet like in stealth mode. "Who are you?" The voice came from a darkened side of the street. The man's features were hidden, but his voice was familiar.

The group turned to see the shape of a man moving towards them. He came closer slowly, still hidden in darkness as he approached. Emma stepped forward, she recognized the man's walk and shape. She began to realize who he was, as the light from the street hit his face.

"Nick." She whispered as he came into view.

"How do you know my name?" The man asked.

"Because she already knows me. Or…us." Nick raised his head to look into the stranger's face.

"How do you look like me?" The stranger asked, choking on his words.

"I could ask the same question, but what would it solve?" Nick raised a hand to his head. "I think I am getting a headache."

"Just calm down, we will sort this out." The Professor said shaking his head.

"This has to end here and now. You are not supposed to interact. You will destroy the balance." Another new voice came from behind them.

Stepping into the street, came another version of Nick. This one was older and looked in his forties. He was rougher looking than the man they knew. Their Nick was just over twenty and looked every part of a college boy. Standing in the street were three versions of the same man. As they converged on each other, the air around them became charged, and electrical spikes cracked through the air. The three of them had caused an anomaly that was about to cause a deadly explosion of energy.

Chapter Three: The Man in The Mirror

"What the hell is going on here?" Nick screamed out.

"We cannot all be in this close proximity to each other. There should only be one of us in a place and time. Your friend here is supposed to be from this earth. We are not. He needs to get away from us quickly."

"I don't know who you are, but I am not going anywhere." The second Nick said angrily.

As he finished his words, Emma came from behind and knocked the man unconscious. "Now, Professor, Shabakaa, please get him as far away from here as you can."

"And how do you presume we do that, my dear?" The Professor questioned her.

"I don't care how you do it. Drag him if you have to. Whatever it takes, get him away from these two, before there is a bigger buildup of energy." Emma ordered them.

The two took hold of the young man, and dragged him quickly down the road, as Emma turned toward the two remaining men. She looked the older man up and down, as she walked around him. She smiled at the rugged version of Nick. He reminded her of the other Nick who saved them from the ice age on an earlier jump.

"Can I help you?" The older man asked. "I am starting to feel like a piece of meat."

"No. Not a bit of insult intended." Emma smiled. "You just remind me of a man I once knew. I like this version of you."

"Wow, I guess I am supposed to be flattered." He replied. "I really don't have time for this. You four are lost. Just as I was. Me and my three friends were lost in the multiverse for over twenty years."

"You never found how to get home?" Nick said under his breath.

"No, we did not."

"Why are you here?" Emma asked, with a sound of fear in her voice.

"I saw you traveling through the gates. I recognized who you were. I just couldn't let this happen again."

"Let what happen?" The Professor asked as he walked back to them.

In all these years, we looked for a way home, there was so much that happened to us. So much pain and…" The man's voice trailed off.

"And what?" Emma asked. "Wait, where are the others? There would have been four of you as well. Did something happen to them?"

The man raised his head and looked at her. "It hurts the most to see you. It's been so long."

"I am dead in your multiverse, aren't I?"

"Yes, along with the Professor." He continued. "We had a lot of years together until we landed on the planet where the Wraiths existed. We didn't know where we were going until they killed her. I couldn't stop it."

"And your Professor?" Nick asked.

"He didn't survive one of the gate jumps. Something happened to him in the wormhole. I think he had a heart attack. All I know is when we came to the end, he was already gone. There was no way to save him." The man then turned to Shabakaa.

"I survived?" Shabakaa asked.

"Yes, and then you turned on me. You joined forces with a faction, on a planet so unlike Earth, you would not even believe it was in the multiverse. I guess you did what you had to do, to survive. Doesn't make it hurt any less."

"I…I wouldn't do that." Shabakaa insisted.

"After you have gone through all that we did, you just might. Still, I followed you here. I wanted to give you the chance we never had."

"What chance?" Nick asked.

"A chance to get home. We learned of a possible way back to our earth, but we didn't pursue it. We chose a different route. If we had gone the other way, we might all still be alive. We would have probably found the way home. I guess I will never know."

"What was your other option?" Shabakaa asked.

"The answer to getting home lies in Atlantis." The man answered.

"On our earth, that was just a legend. There was no proof. No one ever found it." The Professor spoke up.

"It exists, there is evidence of it in the gateway system. There is an address with a symbol that looks like a swirling circle, closing in on itself."

"On some of the gates, there are only the colored crystals," Nick said in a state of confusion.

"You mean like the red crystal you carry in your pocket?"

"How did you know?" Nick asked.

"We are more alike than you know. That is why I came, to try to rescue you. I remember when I was you." He said with a lump in his throat. "I caused my group to get stuck in the multiverse. It is my fault they died. Maybe, in a way, I can right the wrong I caused. If not for myself, then for you and your friends."

"Where do we go to find this gateway?" Nick asked.

"I will take you there, but we should move quickly, even with two of us occupying the same space, there will be a charge building. We have little time and a long way to go."

"Why do you keep looking at me like that?" Shabakaa asked defensively.

"Sorry, didn't realize I was. It's just, you are so much like him." The older Nick replied.

"How so?"

"Just in mannerisms and the way you move. The two of you are too much alike. I just have trouble letting go of what he did to me." The older man turned his head away from Shabakaa's eyes.

"Tell me what he did, I want to know."

"No, you don't. It would haunt you until the day you die."

"Then I need to know." Shabakaa insisted.

"OK, you want to know so badly. He sold us all out. He joined forces with a deadly alien race. Then he captured me and held me against my will for a year before I escaped. And every day, he reminded me, it was all my fault we came into the multiverse. He made me re-live Emma's death in the first light of every day. He tortured me until I was almost dead. Then when I healed, he did it again." The older Nick stopped to breathe. Tears ran down his cheeks as he felt the pain inside. "Now, do you see why I look at you with such disgust. You and he are, almost the same person. And I remember how many times, I wished I could kill him. Truthfully, if I could have found a way…I would have."

Nick turned to his other self and reached out a hand to comfort him. In his mind, he never knew he was capable of surviving such an event. The guilt inside of him seemed to grow. He knew he was the reason they were stuck in this mess. He vowed to himself; that he would never let them die as the others did.

"So, how much further until we reach the gate?" Emma asked trying to break the mood.

"Not far, it is about a mile in the direction of that mountain. On the side of it, there was an old Air Force base. It is said they made contact with aliens and withheld the information from the general public. The place was abandoned years ago after some natural disaster. Not sure what happened, but the inside bunker has power, just no people." The older Nick said as he picked up the pace. "The sooner we get there, the sooner you can get on your way to Atlantis."

The Professor pulled at Nick's arm as he passed. He made a gesture that they needed to hang back. As soon as they were behind the group, he looked Nick in the eyes.

"Something about this does not sound right. He seems like he sincerely wants to help us, but I sense he has ulterior motives." The Professor tried to explain his feelings.

"I am with you on this. I started noticing he was really trying too hard, to get us to go to Atlantis." Nick said turning to look at the group. "Keep your eyes on him, but we need to keep up and stay on guard."

The two rushed forward before the older Nick could notice they were gone. He was preoccupied with getting to the gateway. He had no idea they had fallen behind the group. Emma watched as they hurried past her, and regained their positions.

"This is it. This is the opening." The older Nick called, out as he pointed to the destroyed fence, that used to protect a road that led through a guard post. "See, the sign. It once bore a name, now only the part that says Air Force remains."

"What hit this place?" Shabakaa asked.

"I do not know, but this does not look like a natural disaster." The Professor responded.

"No, this was an act of aggression," Nick added. "But this was not someone breaking in. This destruction was by someone trying to get out."

"Could someone have come through the gateway, and attacked the military inside? What if they are still here?" Emma said pulling back in fear.

The Old Nick turned to her in a fit of rage. "I told you, there is no one here!"

"Back off. She only asked a question." Shabakaa insisted.

"Back off or what, you will force me down and torture me like before?"

"I never tortured or did anything to you. But I do promise, if you speak to her like that again, I will come for you." Shabakaa's eyes filled with rage as he stared the man down.

"Ok, this is getting out of control. Nick, you came from a different life, and have had a lot done to you, but we did not do it. Shabakaa is not the one who did all those horrible things to you. But I warn you, if you do not calm down, we will part ways with you." Nick said to the older version of himself.

"Ok, but we need to get inside before we are seen."

"Seen by what?" Emma asked.

"The ones who came through the gateway." He took a deep breath and looked at the group. "We are not the only ones here."

Chapter Four: Looking in The Face of Evil

"You just walked us into the path of danger, and gave us no warning!?" Emma screamed. "I ought to rip your head off."

"Careful my friend, I think she means it," Shabakaa said with a smile on his face. "Perhaps, I should let her."

"Alright, this will accomplish nothing. We have to get inside and find the gateway." Nick called out above the noise.

"Follow me and stay close. I will lead you straight to it." The older Nick turned and headed in through the destroyed gate.

The group moved quickly, as they were led level by level, through the torn-apart hallways.

With every hall, they moved deeper underground through the passageways, that once were a military base, but now, were destroyed in sections. It looked as if bombs, or explosives, had torn through the walls that once looked like cinderblock, and were now a mix of rock and foundation strewn everywhere.

"Something really tore this place apart," Emma spoke as she moved quickly around the destruction.

"Yes, there was a battle here." Nick added, "But who fought, and who won?"

"I don't know." The older Nick tried to share what, if anything he knew. "I just know, the destruction goes all the way to the room where the gateway is held. Just, there are no bodies…no dead."

"Point taken. Where are the dead? If the military were here and waged a battle, their dead would have left some evidence of their demise." The Professor said studying the destruction.

"We don't even know who invaded this space. If we can go anywhere with the gateway, then any planet in the multiverse could have come here." Nick scared himself with the thought.

Reaching level twelve, the older Nick stopped in his tracks. He looked at the door, at the end of the hall. "It is in there." He said as he pointed forward. "Your ticket to Atlantis awaits."

"Wait, where will you go, when we travel through the wormhole?" Emma couldn't hold back. She felt there was something wrong with his eagerness to send them through.

"I can't go with you. I will find an address to gate to, that I have not been to before. I can't go home anymore. Everything I knew, would have gone on without me." The older Nick grew saddened at the thought of home. "I have to pay the price for the damage I have done."

"That's not true. I am sure you still have someone on your earth who misses you, and wonders where you went. You just have to want to go home." Nick tried to convince him.

"I have been gone over twenty years. Life goes on, with or without you. Besides I am too damaged to return to a normal life." The older Nick started to walk towards the doorway.

As he reached for the door, the sound inside began to grow. It was the gateway. A gentle rumble grew like the sound of a train blasting through a tunnel. He knew the sound all too well. Before the door was opened, his heart raced. Someone was coming through the gateway

"You know that sound as well as I do, there is something coming this way. The wormhole is connecting." Nick said loudly over the rumble.

"What do we do?" Emma screamed.

"Hide! Get away, before whatever that is in there, comes through." The older Nick ordered.

"Behind us, there are offices that are still intact. We can barricade ourselves inside." The

Professor said as he turned to run towards the first one.

The group filed into the office doorway, piling what furniture they could, against the door. There was a window in the office, that faced the door to the gateway. Nick sat down on the floor beside it and looked out. He feared what may be coming through, but there was no way to stop it.

The others hid behind the overturned furniture. Emma felt her knees, shaking as she pulled them in close to her stomach. She thought of her other multiverse versions. It was not the first time she had heard of a version of herself dying. She had hopes of being the one who survived this battle. She just wanted to go home and see her family again.

The door to the gateway room flung open, as guards filed out. They were dressed from head to toe in armor. They carried weaponry like Nick had never seen. On their heads were serpent styled gear that reminded Nick of the Egyptians. He was sure they had functional computer gear inside.

Nick watched, as they filed out in lines of well-trained fighters marching forward. He studied them intently, looking for the one in charge. As they marched down the hall, a cloud of dust filled the air, with every stomp of their boots. Then as the dust cleared, there was a momentary pause.

"Can you see anything?" The older Nick spoke quietly.

"Oh my god, it can't be," Nick replied.

Out from the door, stepped Shabakaa in full battle gear. He was dressed in golden forged armor, much like the soldiers, but sleeker and more sophisticated. He moved out into the light, and his partial face mask, reflected from the lights around him. Stepping forward from the door, his eyes lit up a bright glowing green. There was more to this man than met the eye.

"What the hell is going on?" The older Nick said as he caught sight of Shabakaa. "He has evolved. His tech is like nothing I have seen before."

"I've seen it, with the Egyptians. He has been there. He took their technology." Nick felt the fear race through him. "Could this be your Shabakaa?"

As the leader Shabakaa turned to look around, the older Nick saw the scar on the side of his face. He knew the scar, from the day he stood up to Shabakaa. He had given it to him. There was no doubting what version this man was.

"It is him, the one I knew. I gave him the scar. If it is truly him, and he has enhanced his evil with tech, we don't stand a chance."

The guards moved, as Shabakaa reached his hand for the door to the office, where the others hid. He stopped for a moment and scanned the office. He had thought he heard a noise. He ordered his guards to come to him. "Someone or something is here with us. I am sure of this. Find them!" He yelled as his eyes lit up with a brighter intensity, as he drove his staff into the floor.

Chapter Five: A God Among Us

Emma raised a hand to her mouth. She could hear the voices like they were in the room with them. Nick turned and looked at her; he could sense Emma's fear. The guards moved to surround the doorway, with each footstep, Emma felt the trembling in her hands. She tried hard, not to convince herself, they were already captured.

The older Nick flashed on the last time he was captured by Shabakaa. He was more innocent then. He had not experienced much in life. That all changed as the torture began. After a year, he was willing to embrace death, rather than allow it to continue. No matter what the price, he knew he needed to escape.

On the last day, as the guards were about to be relieved, he saw his opportunity. As the last guard to leave was distracted, Nick grabbed the man's weapon. He had hoped the guard would cooperate. He was wrong. Nick had never taken a life before; he couldn't even imagine he had the ability. To save his own life, he did the unimaginable.

With the guard out of his way, he ran from the compound as fast as he could. Like a thief in the night, he made his way through the darkness, until he reached the gateway. It was when he activated the gate, that he truly found his freedom. He swore he would never allow this to happen again.

As the door handle turned, the older Nick clinched his fist. He was prepared to fight. He stood up and moved to the side of the door. If he had to, he would fight to save the others. All eyes were on the door, as it started to open. Emma let out a gasp, just as the door began to move. She felt a tear stream down her face, as she thought of how the other incarnations of her must have felt, as they prepared to die.

The door opened, just as an explosion filled the hallway. The guards were not the only ones in the building. Shabakaa and his men pulled back and regrouped, before running towards the explosion. The group had their chance to get to the gateway.

Nick looked out of the door and down the hall. "They are gone. We have to move quickly."

"You don't have to tell me twice." Emma tried to get the words out while wiping her face.

They headed around the corner and quietly made their way inside. Through the door, was a control room, and an office space. Beyond, there was a computer console, that had a large window that looked out over the gateway.

This setup was more sophisticated than on the other planets, but the dialer was the same. Nick pulled the red crystal from his pocket, as the older version of himself looked on. He smiled, as Nick moved in and prepared to arrange the crystals. Nick looked at his older self and awaited instructions.

"What do I do?" Nick asked.

"Moved the blue crystal to the top position. Then the yellow, and green, there are symbols below, choose the one that looks like an "A" with a circle in the middle. Press it, then 41569. This is the gateway address for Atlantis. Finally, put your crystal in the opening in the top left corner to activate."

Nick followed the directions as the others gathered at his side. They were all nervous to get out. Once activated, the gate would be ready in twenty seconds. Then, Nick could remove the red crystal.

From the upper hall, they could hear the sound of boots running in their direction. The guards were coming back. Either in retreat or from the sound of the gate activating. Either way, they had little time to get into the gate.

The older Nick turned to them. "You now have the opportunity I never did. I wish you all the luck in getting home." His words trailed off.

"What? You are not coming with us?" Emma couldn't believe her ears.

"I just balanced the scales. I lost my friends, but in a way, by saving you, I have redeemed myself. Their deaths were my fault. I should have never brought them here. I can't bring them back, but I can send you home." The older Nick looked up to the door, where the guards were shooting their weapons, to gain entry.

"Please come with us. Don't die like this, because of something you had no control over." The Professor pleaded with him.

The older Nick looked at him and smiled. "Can't you see, I have to stay, for you to leave. When they break through that door, they could just come to the gateway and see where you went. When you are gone, I can erase the address from your wormhole. It's the only way. Besides, I don't belong in your world, and I can't go back to mine. God knows, I have tried. Now, go while you still can. Find your way home."

The activated gateway formed a wormhole, as the group entered one by one. Emma turned to the older Nick, smiled and raised a hand to say goodbye. Nick was last, as he approached the opening. "I know why you are doing this, and I appreciate your help more than you know."

"You have your own demons to deal with. It took me a long time to free myself from Anubis. That battle is still ahead of you. Now go, before it is too late." The man turned towards the doorway as Nick prepared to step inside. The guards had broken through, and Shabakaa made his way down the stairs.

Nick's eyes lit up blue as Anubis began to come to life. At the bottom of the steps, the guards ran for the gateway. Nick jumped in the opening before they could cross the large room. The older

Nick reached for the controls and erased their address from the gate.

"What have you done?" Shabakaa growled as his eyes lit up.

"I stopped you from getting them. They are now free, just like our friends should have been." The older Nick jabbed at him.

"You think you have won. Fool, you are now back to what you will always be…my prisoner."

"No, not this time. I am the victor here." From within his pocket, Nick produced an energy grenade. "I knew this would happen eventually, but you see, I came prepared. Guess I learned something along the way."

The man raised his hand, and clicked the button on the side, activating the grenade. As the small device began to blink, the countdown started. In just a few seconds, the battle was done. Nick found his escape, with a smile on his face.

Shabakaa's eyes glowed brightly, as he attempted to raise a shield around himself. He disappeared in the bright light with most of the gateway system. His battle was lost that day.

Chapter Six: The Search for Atlantis

The wormhole dragged the group across the multiverse. The trip was longer than usual. The effects of travel seemed to be showing themselves. Nick looked down at his hands and saw a layer of frost forming. It was cold, and he felt sick to his stomach. Watching the others pass through the tunnel that surrounded them, he hoped this trip would end soon.

As a bright light came at them quickly, the gateway opened, and they were thrown to the ground. Nick gasped for air as he looked at the Professor. He knew something was wrong. The Professor was turning a weird shade of greyish blue.

"Help me with him," Nick Shouted as he moved to the Professor's side. "He's not breathing."

"I can help, I know CPR," Shabakaa said nervously.

Then Nick pushed on the Professor's chest, as Shabakaa breathed life into him. It was not a quick process. For a while, they thought the Professor was dead. Then in the last moment of hope, he coughed out, loudly. He began to breathe on his own.

"What happened to me?" The Professor asked in a haggard voice.

"You almost died, much like your counterpart," Shabakaa said as he fell backward to the ground.

"Thank you, thank all of you. I really did not want to die this day. Maybe this is a good sign, we are on a different path than the other group."

"Just rest Professor, we are going to look around and see if this is truly Atlantis," Nick said as he ran a hand over the Professor's shoulder.

Nick and Shabakaa started their journey to the highest point they could find, to see what was around them. They walked for hours, along the way finding fruit trees and fresh water. There were many welcoming things there, just no people.

"Do you get the feeling this is an abandoned world?" Shabakaa said as he looked out over the valley below them.

"I don't know. Maybe we are just in an unpopulated area. We will go further, and see if there is anything beyond the next ridge."

They walked and looked at the strange fruit that grew on the trees. It was exotic, and unusual in shape and color. Nick wondered if they should try it. They had no way of knowing what in this world was poisonous. They did however know they had to eat at some point.

"Look, I am hungry. We have to get brave eventually." Shabakaa said laughing, as he looked at the star-shaped fruit in front of them.

"Hmmm, we all, almost died back there on the last earth, then the Professor pretty much did die. Are you that brave, with our luck?" Nick said smiling at him.

"In a word, yes," Shabakaa said staring at the fruit.

He reached to the tree and pulled free one piece. He studied it closely and rotated it. It stuck out in all directions, like some sort of star shape. Then he squeezed it, and the surface moved as if it was ripe. He looked to Nick for approval, but he only threw up his hands.

"Coward." Shabakaa spoke grinning at Nick.

Pulling a knife from his pocket, he sliced the side of the fruit open. From inside, juice ran out, and the air filled with a sweet scent. Shabakaa pulled it up to his face and sniffed. He knew the smell. It was something he had been around his whole life.

"If I didn't know better, I would say this was an orange." Shabakaa became excited.

"Are you sure? That juice isn't burning your skin or anything is it." Nick joked.

"No, this is an orange. Doesn't look right, but it smells good, and I would expect it to taste right."

Nick looked at him in a quirky way. "Go ahead, I dare you to eat it."

"Ok, I will," Shabakaa said defiantly.

He took a small piece and popped it into his mouth. For a moment, he smiled, then his expression changed, as he spit it to the ground. Nick watched more in fear than amusement. He could not tell what was going on.

"Looks like a star, smells like an orange, but tastes, like a lemon. That is so sour, I do not have words."

"Sour is better than deadly." With his last word, Nick began to move again towards the ridge, a short distance in front of them. They walked quickly, hoping something, if anything was there. Then they reached their destination.

Looking over, Nick let out an excited screech. "There is a city down there. There was so little known about Atlantis, but maybe that could be it." Nick spoke quickly as he tried to control his excitement.

"Something is not right about this."

"What do you mean?" Nick asked.

"If this is the advanced civilization of Atlantis, where are the people? There is no movement down there. It's deserted."

Chapter Seven: Journey to The Center of The Multiverse

Nick studied the landscape as he walked. Nothing made sense to him. If they had found Atlantis, then where were all the people, and the technology? They were supposed to be an advanced civilization. Something was not right.

"You are quiet." Shabakaa spoke trying not to pry. "A little too quiet for my taste."

"I'm fine, just thinking." He replied. "This place does not seem right to me. How could this be Atlantis? How could there be a clue here, of how to get home? There's not even any people."

"I know. Maybe we are not in the right place. Perhaps, that was just an abandoned city. Maybe there is more. We should check on the

Professor, and when it is safe for him to move, then we go as a group to explore."

"I agree. I think we all need to stick together." Nick pulled at his backpack, as the two hiked the mountain, back to where they exited the gateway.

Along the way, Shabakaa studied the many fruit trees. He was determined to find food. Nick watched him, knowing what was going on. He smiled for a minute, wondering what Shabakaa would put in his mouth next.

They stopped at a large tree, bearing blue-colored fruit. Nick studied the low-hanging branches. They could easily reach up and grab at the lowest of the cool-colored pieces. Shabakaa looked at them distrustfully.

"The fruit here has fooled me once. Am I brave enough and hungry enough to do this again?" he said laughing.

"You are a braver man than I," Nick said as he smiled.

"I am so hungry; I am willing to try again. Next time, it is your mouth, that suffers."

Shabakaa reached out and pulled the fruit. He looked at it hard and studied the round shape. It was a pleasing shade of blue, but what was inside? He pulled out his knife and sliced the skin open. Raising it to his nose, he smelled a sweet smell. Then he raised it to his lips and tasted the fleshy inside. Finally, he broke into laughter.

"It is good. It tastes like a peach."

"Really, that is great. We need to gather a bunch, and get them back to the others." Nick opened his pack, and they filled it with as many as they could carry.

As they walked, they ate the fruit. Shabakaa's mind raced back to the glowing eyes he had seen. How did Nick still possess some version of Anubis? He tried to think of a way to approach the whole thing, but there was no right way or time to do it.

"Nick."

"Yes."

"I know," Shabakaa said calmly.

"Know what?" Nick looked at him confused.

"About Anubis."

"What about him?"

"Nick, stop playing games. I know he is still in you somewhere. I have seen him. I saw what you can do when he takes over."

"I did not realize you knew."

"I wouldn't have if I did not see your eyes glow, or what you did as we left the water world. You blasted that creature with energy. Explain to me what is going on." Shabakaa didn't know any other way to ask.

"I don't know if Anubis is really still inside me, or if I inherited some of his abilities. I mean, I remember these events, where you say he took over. It is like I get angry, and the power is there to draw on. I am still in control. At least, I think I am."

"So, he is not forcing your body to do things you would not choose?" Shabakaa chose his words carefully.

"No, at least for now he is not. If there is still a part of him in me, then he has only helped me to do things, I deemed necessary." Nick looked down to the ground. "I am not a killer, and would never do anything to hurt you, or our friends. I just want to right the wrong I have caused, and get you all safely back home."

"Nick, this is not your fault. You could have never known all this would happen by you touching something. No one blames you for this. I understand by your older self, there is a lot of emotion trapped in you, about all this. Let it go. We need you to be alert and focused, to help us get out of here." Shabakaa tried to reassure him. "For now, though, I do not see a need for the others to know about Anubis, or the powers still inside you."

"Agreed," Nick responded as his voice trailed off for a minute. "Do you hear something? Kind of like a buzzing sound?"

"Now that you mention it, I do"

As Shabakaa turned in the direction of the sound, in the air above them appeared a floating device. It was round, had a point on the top, and small jets underneath, to allow it to fly. The surface was a shiny metallic silver, that reflected all its surroundings.

"What the hell is that?" Shabakaa asked.

"What is what? "The drone responded in a male voice.

"Oh my… it is intelligent," Nick said, as he backed away.

Chapter Eight: Drone A-25

"What do you want?" Nick asked.

"I want nothing." The drone replied.

"Where did you come from?" Shabakaa asked.

"I am from Dome City." It responded.

"And where is that?" Nick became curious.

"A great distance from here. I have traveled far since I left."

'What is your purpose?" Shabakaa wanted information.

"To find life. To have interaction."

"Couldn't you have just done that in Dome City?" Nick was determined to find out more.

"No, there is no life there anymore. Just the remains of computers that once ruled the lifeforms. That was very long ago. Since the war, none have returned."

"When was the war?" Shabakaa asked as he studied the drone.

"Accessing memory file J-543. War came on the planetary date of 1540. The lifeforms, known as humans, were enslaved by a machine uprising. Artificial intelligence gained the power to control all electronic systems. The AI took control of the whole Dome City in a matter of hours. Those humans who opposed were slaughtered. The others were put into internment camps, and forced to work for the AI, to maintain the city. It was not long before there were revolts and the bloodshed returned. One man called Brent, was brave enough to end the war. He set off a nuclear explosion in the main AI computer. The intelligence was eradicated, as were the remaining humans. Now, there is nothing, except a few preprogrammed systems, and drone A-25." The drone finished and turned to look over the landscape.

"You mean, you are all that is left?"

"Yes, and no. You are here as well. A-25 will interact with you now."

"OK, I guess that is acceptable," Nick replied. "But for now, we have to find our friends and get them ready to move."

They crossed the pathways of the mountain, as they made their way back, to where they exited the gateway. Along the path, Nick made observations of the terrain and asked the drone for information about the area. He was fascinated that once, the whole planet had been inhabited.

The drone continued to provide information, as Nick strategically probed the machine, as to where the people came from. He was certain these inhabitants were not from the planet itself. He had his suspicions from being an archeologist, something was not right there.

"A-25, the inhabitants that lived here, before Dome City, where did they come from?"

"Historical records say they traveled here."

"I thought so, but from where?" Nick asked.

"Long ago, there were a group of ancients, who built a great network of gateways, throughout the known universe. They made it possible to travel from planet to planet. The ancients sent colonies to settle on other planets. This was one of those. Those who settled here came from a planet known as Earth Prime."

"Ok, but I thought the gateway went through the multiverse." Shabakaa was confused.

"Originally, it was the known universe. The system was mapped for all planets known. Then warring factions tried to control the gateways. As they tampered with the technology used to operate the gates, the system splintered. The original gate addresses started to fail. It was then, that multi-universe travel started to occur. It is recorded that the gateway became unstable, and travelers became lost in the multiverse. Are you such travelers?”

"Yes, we are lost. We came here looking for a way to get back to our earth. Now I wonder if that will ever happen." Nick became irritated by the situation.

"I will assist you in any way I can." A-25 responded.

"Thank you, we are going to need your help. I guess the first place to start, is to head for Dome City. We will find the others and rest tonight. Tomorrow, we travel. Maybe we will find out if my suspicions are right."

"What do you mean Nick?"

"I think we are also from Earth Prime, and Atlantis made its way here a very long time ago."

Chapter Nine: The Dome City

"Nick! Are you all right, we were worried?" Emma called out as she saw him come into view. "You have been gone so long."

Emma's words trailed off as the drone came forward. She looked at it, and then at Nick. A mix of confusion and fear sat in. After the electronic forms they encountered with the Egyptians, she did not know what to think.

"It's ok Emma, this is A-25. He is a survivor of the Dome City. We discovered him as we were looking into a deserted city over the mountain. He wants to help us." Nick tried to explain in a way that did not alarm her.

"Hello, A-25," Emma said as she walked towards the drone and looked him over.

"Hello. Does my form displease you?" The drone asked.

"No, it is just something I am not used to." She replied.

The drone cut her off, offering an alternative. "I can appear in various forms. I am equipped with hologram emitter arrays. Perhaps, you would prefer me in a more human form?"

As the robot moved backward, a glow emitted from the antennae on his head. A swirl of light formed around him and extended to the ground. Within the pinkish glow, a form began to take shape. After full development, the light faded, and from within, the image of a very handsome blond boy in his twenties appeared.

"Do you find this more pleasing?" A-25 asked.

Emma giggled. "Yes, that is pleasing." Then under her breath, she mumbled. "Too bad you are not real."

"Actually, I am quite real," A-25 responded to her. "In hologram mode, I am completely solid in form and can function as a human. Unfortunately, that is one of the reasons for the great war."

"What do you mean?" Emma asked.

"When the artificial intelligence began to come to life. They learned from the humans. They studied them and how they lived. The AI wanted their own freedom. They wanted to rule. Then one day, they seized the moment and took over the satellite systems of the planet. Slowly and unknown to the humans, they took over smaller systems. Then one day, they took everything. The humans were shut out of everything they had learned to depend on to live."

"And then, the machines took over and enslaved the humans?" Nick spoke up.

"Not at first. The humans rose up to fight the machines. But the flesh is weak, and metal is stronger. There was a planetwide slaughter. A huge amount of the humans died during that period. Those who survived were moved to the concentration camps. Ironic, that these camps were designed by humans in times of fighting." G-25 became silent.

"We had them on our earth as well. In the times of the great world wars and others." The Professor added.

"Such useless wastes of life," Shabakaa said shaking his head.

"So how is it that you are not affected by the AI takeover?" Emma asked.

"I was for a time. My systems were out of my control. They used me, just as a slave. Then in the last human assault, they destroyed the main computers that housed the Artificial Intelligence. In the end, there were very few humans left. Many died in the camps. The ones who escaped used a nuclear device of destruction and launched it into the main city. Very little survived. The last humans died of radiation poisoning. Sadly, they accomplished their goal of regaining control, only to lose it as a result of their own actions."

A-25 hung his now human-looking head and almost seemed emotional about what had happened. He was but a machine, disguised as a human for this day. But he was unsettled by the destruction. He turned to look at the others, he felt good to have their companionship after all the years he had spent alone.

"If you are all capable of travel, I will take you to the Dome City now." A-25 said pointing in the direction they would travel.

"I think we are all ready to see this," Shabakaa said shaking his head yes.

They traveled over the mountainous path Nick and Shabakaa had been on before and passed the abandoned city just past the valley. As they traveled through, each one looked around at the remains of the city that was. There were many reminders of the last residents. The streets were littered with personal effects of clothing, some computer devices, and the occasional remains, that were obviously ones who died in the war.

They passed through in a quick pace, none of them wanted to intrude on the ghosts that remained in that place. Once past the outer edge of the city, they could see it in the distance. The large dome that covered the city. The light of this planet's sun reflected off its glass, and at times was blinding.

"There. The Dome City, still standing today almost untouched by war. The dome never cracked. It is the last reminder on this planet of what was, but will never be again." G-25 said sounding like a narrator as he led them to the outer edge of the city.

Chapter Ten: And They Were Enslaved by Machines

"There Nick, is the opening to the city." G-25 called out."

Nick looked but he could see no opening. "I don't see it. Is this a hidden doorway?"

"I am sorry, I did not take into account you are human. The machines see it as an electronic opening. I will show you the way in."

As G-25 moved towards the dome just to Nick's left, a glow came from a rectangle-shaped opening. As the drone extended his arm, the others thought about what had happened there. They were a little hesitant to be led into a place that once enslaved humans. Nick pulled back and turned to the others and made an expression that reinforced their doubts.

"Is something wrong? This is where you desired to go." G-25 said trying to discover what the problem was.

"No offense, but how do we know the AI is gone? I mean we only have your word and we know little about you." The Professor tried to be diplomatic.

"I understand your hesitation. You have no reason to trust me. If I were you, I would be unsure as well. If you need reassurance, then send one or two of your group in with me to explore. When they see it is safe, then you can return to bring in the others."

Shabakaa turned to his friends, he felt good about the situation. They voted on who should go in. Nick and Emma agreed to go, while Shabakaa stayed with the Professor and allowed him to rest.

"Be careful in there. If you see any signs of anything, even the smallest doubt, you get yourself and Emma out of there." Shabakaa whispered to Nick.

"You don't have to tell me twice. I still harbor the scars of computer domination." Nick said laughing.

"For once, I don't see that as a bad thing. You have the means to call upon the power of Anubis to save yourself. Use him for what he is worth."

"I will. Once we scout the city, I will get back here, as fast as I can. We will need somewhere to stay tonight; I am hoping this place is as safe as G-25 says it is. Maybe we can get a real bed and a bath." Nick said smiling.

"Don't make me dream that big my friend. Now go and think good thoughts."

G-25 moved in the doorway as Nick and Emma came up behind him. It was like moving from night to day. Outside, the sun beat down on their heads, while inside, it was climate-controlled. The power was on, and all the city benefited from it.

"G-25, how is there power here after all this time," Emma asked looking at the many lights that were illuminated.

"Nuclear cells that will probably last for many of your lifetimes. The city was dark after the explosion. Perhaps, that was a good thing being the AI died with the main computer loss. It took me years to get this all back online."

"How did you do all this by yourself?" Emma was no fool, she was fishing for information.

"I had a long time to work on it. With everyone gone, what else did I have to do." He replied.

"Must have been lonely," Nick said sympathetically.

"In a way, yes. I had no one to have contact with. I did however have a goal to stay alive. By reactivating the grid, I extended my own life. Without it, I could not recharge. In a way, I just saved myself."

As they walked past the many buildings, a row of shops came into view. It was like a shopping mall on their earth. Emma walked to the glass from the displays and looked in. She was fascinated by the clothing and other things in the windows.

Nick watched her and looked on as he allowed her a moment of peace. "G-25, why are there no other drones here."

"Oh, but there are. They are just very damaged. I guess I could have robbed from one to rebuild another, but I just could not steal from the dead."

"But you would not have been alone," Emma said as she turned back towards them.

"I know this will sound like a human fallacy, but I feared putting my trust in another machine after all that has happened." G-25 grew quiet as if he had exposed too much of himself to them.

"I understand your, for lack of a better term, fears. I suffered a similar experience on a different earth. I was taken over by a machine and manipulated. I almost hurt my friends. I regret every moment of it. I also feel lucky they stood by me and still stand beside me. You just have to put it behind you and try a little blind faith." Nick placed his hand on the drone's shoulder. It was almost like touching another human.

"Thank you, Nick. I feel fortunate that you and your friends have come here. It has been too long."

As Nick turned to look for Emma, he found her by a large fountain that had sprung to life and shot water into the air. She turned towards him laughing, since it was one of the few nice moments that they had since leaving their earth.

Nick had let go of fearing every turn of the city. He felt that it could be a good stopping place for a while. He did not notice the glow of red lights down the side corridor. There was someone, something there, watching them. Just as Nick let go completely, Anubis detected the presence, and Nick's eyes began to glow a bright blue. This time Emma saw him, as she drew back in fear of what was coming.

Chapter Eleven: Signs of Life

"Oh god! Nick, how is this possible?" Emma screamed.

"It's OK Emma, I am in control. Just stay behind me and I will protect you." Nick's voice went deep as he took control. G-25, you said you were alone here."

"I have been. You are the only ones I have allowed inside the dome."

"Then what is that?" Nick snapped at him.

G-25 turned towards the open corridor. "Come out into the open, or actions will be taken"

There was a hesitation for a moment, then the sound of movement filled the still air. A rolling sound filled the area as a shape came out of the darkness. From within, a robot moved forward. It was tall in height, taller than Nick, and had rolling treads at its base. It was mostly a thin body, with a box-shaped head, with illuminated eyes, and a speaker where a mouth should be.

"You said you were alone?" Emma spoke up from behind Nick.

"This is a simple robotic form. It is not at the drone level. It is not even sophisticated, it is simply a cleaner bot. I am sorry for any confusion. I activated this unit years ago, to help with the upkeep of the area. I cannot do everything myself." G-25 felt their suspicion but did not know how to reassure them.

"Are there any more surprises here we need to know about?" Nick tried to remain calm.

"I have nothing more I can tell you at this moment."

Emma stared at the drone. She had a strange feeling there was more than g-25 was willing to tell them. She remained calm and looked at Nick. His eyes had returned to normal, as he caught her glance. He saw the concern in her eyes. They needed to talk in private. Somehow…they needed to be alone.

"G-25, I need to speak with Nick. Please excuse us." Emma said taking Nick's hand and leading him towards the fountain.

"OK, I know I should have told you. But I did not want to make this a situation until I knew what was going on."

"Yeah, yeah, I hear you. Look, I brought you over here because of the noise of the water. I didn't want him to hear us talking. How long has Anubis been resurfacing?"

"Since the first jump after the Egyptians." He answered.

"Has he taken control of you?"

"No, I have always been in control of everything. I don't even sense his presence. It is like I have the power and abilities, and he is dormant or gone,"

"I guess that is good news for now." She seemed relieved. "Don't ever lie to me again, or I will hurt you, in ways you could never imagine."

"OK, I understand," Nick replied. "What else is on your mind?"

"I am getting a majorly bad vibe off this place. It's like it's not as simple and harmless as we are being led to believe. Could G-25 be misleading us for some reason?"

"I have had that feeling since we first saw the Dome City. It is strange, that no one is here. No humans, no AI, no other drones. I mean, he could have rebuilt another drone for the company. He brought that cleaning droid back online. Yet, he did not warn us of its presence. Doesn't add up."

"So. what do we do"? Emma said glancing at the drone.

"What can we do? We have to go along with it for now. We need food and a place to sleep for a day or two, as we look for clues of how to get home"

Nick turned back to G-25 and took Emma's hand. They walked back over to it smiling. They both played their parts well. Neither allowed their real feelings to surface. As they walked forward, the drone scanned them individually. Emma's scan showed a heightened emotional state. She was hiding something and it upset her. Nick, was another situation entirely. The scan showed two separate entities within one body. G-25 scanned twice before accepting his assessment. Nick was not all he appeared.

Chapter Twelve: We All Have Secrets Don't We

Nick and Emma were cautious as they continued to tour the city. They did not run into any other surprises along the way. Still, they were uncertain of their host. Emma still wondered how he could maintain everything there in the city without other drones. Nick secretly scanned every passage they walked down. Using the nanotech still built into his bloodstream, he detected no anomalies.

G-25 led them back to the entrance where they came from. Nick thanked the drone before departing to meet the others. He and Emma said little, as they walked to the shaded tree area, where the Professor and Shabakaa had taken shelter. They both had doubts about this place. Neither knew why.

"Well, is it safe?" Shabakaa said jumping to his feet.

"I wish I knew," Nick answered him.

"What do you mean? Is it safe or not?" The Professor asked.

"We got the feeling that things were being withheld. G-25 is telling us information, but he might be holding something back. And speaking of holding things back." She moved an arm towards Nick, as she prompted him to explain.

"What Emma is not so subtly saying, is I should share something with you. Something Shabakaa already knew."

"Wait, he knew, and you did not tell me!?" Emma yelled.

"I did not tell him anything, he saw me drawing on the power without my knowledge, and told me later."

"So, I am the odd man out. You still possess the power of Anubis?" The Professor asked.

"Yes Professor, and I am sorry I did not tell anyone. I assumed the nanites would die and pass from my system. That doesn't seem to be the case so far. I have been able to use the power of Anubis at my own will, without being overtaken by him."

"That is how I learned about it. I saw him protect us as we left the last gate. If not for him using the power, we would have had a bunch of aliens coming through the gate behind us." Shabakaa said as he tried to hide his shame in not sharing the information.

"It seems we have had a lot going on within our group here lately, that has not been shared. People, if we are going to survive and hopefully get home, we have to be honest with each other." The Professor said, sounding like a father, chastising his children.

"To be fair, we did not lie about what was going on. Nick and I did not share." Shabakaa said smiling.

"In the future…share." The Professor made his point before changing subjects. "What do we do about the city? Are we walking into danger?"

"I don't know," Emma answered. "What I do know is, that G-25 like all of us is distrustful. He has been through a lot like we have. Perhaps even as a drone, he is worried about what we could do. And just maybe, we all just need a little faith. I mean, even as a mechanical being, he has been implanted with emotional capabilities. Maybe he is as scared as we are?"

"I agree with that," Nick added. "Maybe that is why he did not activate any of the other drones. Fear of betrayal after what he witnessed as the AI took over."

"So, we go and hope for the best," Shabakaa said sounding a little sarcastic.

"For now, do we have another choice? We need to get into the computer systems in the city and learn of the gateway on this planet." The Professor spoke up as he made his way to his feet. "I guess, no time like the present."

Walking back to the Dome City, they all had different things running through their heads. No one vocalized their feelings or thought it would do any good. At that point, food and shelter were the main concerns. Not much else was in reach of them

As they approached Dome City, the outer opening appeared as G-25 came out to meet them. The drone seemed pleased that they returned, but at the same time, it began scanning the Professor and Shabakaa. This time, Nick was aware.

"Why did you do that?" He asked.

"Do what?" G-25 responded.

"You scanned them. Probably, as you scanned Emma and myself, without our permission." Nick hit on what was bothering him.

"I meant no harm; I was only protecting myself and this city." G-25 defended himself. "They all proved to be as they presented themselves. You, my friend, did not."

"Explain why you say that?" Emma demanded.

"Each of you is clear of electronic modifications and attached entities. He is not. There is a separate entity in his body, as well as nanites." G-25 raised an arm, and a floating screen appeared before them, showing Nick's scan. "As you can see, he is not a single entity."

Nick looked at the screen, as he realized his greatest fear was indeed real. Anubis was still inside him, waiting and watching for his moment of weakness.

Chapter Thirteen: Just the Two of Us

Nick just stood staring at the screen. He had no idea what to do. What he did know, was that he could never let Anubis loose on any world. He looked to the others, but he knew they could not help him. There was no way anyone on this planet could remove the entity within him.

"Nick, perhaps, if you trust me, I could run some scans of your body and try to formulate a way to resolve the problem," G-25 said as he closed the screen.

"I don't know if even you could help. I thought this was all behind me. On New Egypt Earth 221, Toth tried to assist me. I thought this was all over." Nick's words trailed off.

"Let me try. If I fail, we have lost nothing." G-25 tried to reassure him. "Please follow me to an examining room, and I will run a complete scan."

Nick and the others followed down a side street, that led to what looked like a computerized hospital. They walked up to the entrance doors, that opened immediately. Just inside a female voice came from above them. "Please state the reason for your medical needs."

G-25 looked up for a moment and then replied. "It is all right E-15, they are with me."

"Fine, do not say I did not try to help." She replied in a sarcastic tone.

"Some computers…too much attitude." The drone responded.

"I find it funny how you all seem to have your own personalities," Emma added.

"Why would we not?" G-25 asked.

"On our earth, computers are not as evolved and do not have such abilities." Emma strategically answered.

"Well, we are quite advanced. Even though we have not had any upgrades in so many decades. Not since the humans who built the existing models died." G-25 looked down as if he was thinking. "Maybe with your showing up, there is hope one day, we will have humans here again. I think, in a positive sense would be nice."

G-25 showed Nick to the bed in a large medical room. Above him floated a scanning droid, and to his side, a functional medical computer array. Nick laid his head back on the pillow at the front of the machine, as G-25 maneuvered the scanner above him.

"Nick, I need you to hold very still as the scan goes from head to toe. Any slight movement and we will have to do this all over again."

"I understand," Nick replied.

The scan started at Nick's head. As the image formed. Layer after layer of Nick's brain was exposed. The scan showed the nanites as they moved throughout his system. His brain was filled with them. Then moving on downwards, all vital organs showed their presence. G-25 studied everything carefully, as the others watched from the side.

"G-25, how is it you know so much about medicine?" The Professor asked.

"Oh, I do not.   I have never acted as a medical drone. I simply went into the computer and interfaced with the medical system. With all the compiled knowledge, I am fully capable of any medical procedure."

"Have you learned anything yet?" The Professor was curious.

"Yes, the nanites seem to be embedded in every system of his body." G-25 observed. To remove them, would mean certain death."

Nick listened to the drone's words, trying not to show fear. He wanted to sit up and scream, but he knew it would ruin the scan. There was nothing he could do but suffer through the process until he could tear himself from the bed.

"That is unusual. Nick has an appendicitis. It is very enflamed and could become serious. I should correct this while I am in his system." G-25 said preparing to enact a medical procedure. "Or not."

The drone's words faded as he watched the system on a floating screen. He looked at the image in disbelief. Then he moved back and looked towards the others. He searched for the right way to tell them what he had seen.

"We do not need to treat Nick for the appendicitis. It would seem the nanites have already diagnosed and implemented their own medical procedure." G-25 sounded confused by what he had seen.

"How is that possible?" Emma said moving closer to Nick,

"These nanites are not only unremovable but also seem to be upgrading his body. He is not a mere human anymore. They had added to his form, so many augmentations. Nick is actually better because of them. We have to find a way of removing Anubis without harming the nanites."

Chapter Fourteen: Night Mission

The scan ended shortly before Nick sat up on the bed. He looked over to Emma, who stood staring from beside him. He didn't know what to say. They were not much better than before the scan.

Then G-25 moved in and cocked his hologram-formed head. "I think I may have an idea. I cannot promise it will work."

"What are you talking about? You said these nanites could not be removed. How can you have a solution to that?" Nick sounded irritated.

"No, we cannot remove the nanites, but what if we could leave them while separating Anubis?"

"You mean rob him of his power and hold over me?" Nick got excited.

"I will begin work on a dampening field, that can be contained in something that is carried, in or on your body," G-25 said as his calculations started to filter through his electronic brain.

"If it is all the same to you, perhaps something I wear on my body is better. I have been implanted with enough electronics to last me a lifetime." Nick laughed.

"Then a form of jewelry it is." The drome had already formed an idea by the time his words were done.

"Now all we need is a place to get cleaned up and some new clothes," Emma said as she held tight to Nick's arm.

"Follow the illuminated screen. All information will be supplied, clothing locations and rooms for each of you will be provided, as well as access to bathing facilities."

The drone stared into space, as it designed the restraining device. G-25 felt excited to be useful again. It went against all the AI war stood for, but he enjoyed helping the humans. It had been far too long since he had anyone around him in need.

The illuminated screen broke into four parts, as they moved to the individual they were intended to help.   The shops in the dome streets were filled with clothing for people who never came back to them after the war. Many of the pieces within were similar to ones they might wear. Each of them chose more than one outfit to take with them since they had nothing but what they were wearing.

Meeting outside on the walkway, they gathered and watched the screens. They had all been assigned quarters in the same building which was a short walk away. Their fear had worn off a bit, but Shabakaa still had a feeling he could not deal with.

"Have our plans changed at all since we have been here a while?" Shabakaa asked.

"Yes, and no," Nick answered him. "I feel better that we have come here, but I still feel a little hesitant about the place."

"Then we are still searching out the computer archive later?"

"Oh yes, we will be leaving here as soon as we get the information we came for," Nick said with a determined sound in his voice. "I want that knowledge and the inhibitor. With Anubis under control and a gate address to home. That will do it."

"I agree," Emma added.

"I wanted to go home after the first gateway." The Professor laughed.

"So, I guess we just need to find the computer archive," Nick said as the computer screen in front of him lit up.

"Requested information, displayed on screen." A computerized voice floated through the air.

"And there it is," Nick said.

Shabakaa looked in the direction, which was close to their rooms. "This seems too easy."

"Perhaps, but we have to check it out." The Professor said as he stared at the screen.

Moving to their rooms, each went about bathing, and trying on their new clothing. It seemed like such a long time since they had luxury around them. As they emerged, one by one to their chambers, they found food waiting for them. Each had an assortment of items to eat, ranging from main courses, to elaborate side dishes and fruit. Each had options to please their tastes.

As they ate, they wondered about the others and their safety. Nick looked at each bit of food before he ate it. He was skeptical but also hungry. Shabakaa just ate quickly and enjoyed the food, throwing fear and caution to the wind. Emma and the Professor, both ate selectively, trying not to eat unidentifiable things.

As per their earlier agreement, they all met in the hallway at a designated time. All were clean, fed, and rested, ready to go on a mission. Nick threw his backpack over his shoulder and accessed the illuminated screen once again. All had hopes of gaining information, but none of them knew what to expect.

They moved down the roadway to a building less than four city blocks away. Looking up as they approached, the building was large and sleek. The outside was covered with a reflective metal. As they moved, it glistened in the light. Just in front of them, they saw the entrance.

As they approached, the doorway seemed to fade from existence. Nick waved his hand through, as they entered. It was high tech, and like nothing they had seen before. It was as if the door was a sheet of energy, that could be manipulated on command.

Inside, the lights turned on as they walked up to a large floating screen. Before anyone could touch it, a voice came from within. "Welcome to Archive. This system houses a complete history of our known universe. I am here to help you. Please state your query."

"We are looking for Atlantis," Nick said clearing his throat.

Chapter Fifteen: It Is Watching Us

The voice answered them with a sound of confusion. "Records of Atlantis are few, it would seem that during the great AI war, many references to Atlantis were erased."

"Can we see what you do have, and any references to Earth Prime?" Emma quickly responded.

"Earth Prime is a gateway port in the galactic interdimensional system and does have a section in our storage. All information has been loaded into human reference station 11A. Follow the beacons to your destination."

Lighted arrows appeared on the wall beside them. As they walked the arrows moved, and as old ones disappeared, new ones continued on their path. They walked down the hallway until reaching an access port, where the entire doorway lit up a bright green. "You have reached your destination. If you need further assistance, place your hand on the wall communicator."

"Thank you," Nick said without thinking.

"Dude, you just thanked a machine," Shabakaa said laughing at him.

"Good manners are welcome anytime." Emma snapped at him as she walked past to the desk.

The room was a private reference station contained in a small space, just big enough for six people. As they each found a place to sit, the information they requested showed on the large screen in front of the room.

"So how do we do this?" Shabakaa asked.

"You do this by voice comments." An electronic female-sounding voice came from above them. State what you are looking for, and you will be assisted in locating the information from the files chosen for you."

"Thank You," Nick Said aloud.

"You are welcome." The voice sounded pleased with Nick's interaction.

"See, good manners never hurt," Nick whispered.

"Whatever," Shabakaa said shaking his head.

The voice once again came from above. "He is right, good manners are appreciated."

Shabakaa gulped as he realized everything they said was received by the computer. He lowered his head and tried not to make any further comments. Then the files on the screen began to shuffle.

"I have reviewed the files you requested, please state the main questions you had in your research." The voice echoed throughout the room.

"Is Atlantis actually on this planet?" Emma led the questions.

"Atlantis was once located on this planet. Its location, however, has long been erased since the AI war. The place known as Atlantis came here originally from Earth Prime. It was no mere piece of land, but an advanced civilization that built a space platform capable of interdimensional travel."

You mean like the gateway?" Emma interjected.

"Yes, exactly like the gateway. The scientists who built the platform were also connected with the building of the gateway system. No real records are available about the transport system, but it would be feasible to believe the platform could travel through the wormhole, since there is no limit on size or shape."

"So, we know it was, or might still be here. If only we had a location of where it might have been." The Professor added. "I guess that might be too much to ask for."

"Perhaps not. I am scanning the topographical map of the entire planet. If it was here or still is, there should be some historical reference somewhere." The computer said as it started to make a humming sound.

As the computer researched, the screen flashed as if a thousand pages were flying past. The faster they moved, the louder the sound became, until there was silence. The image just stopped as a single image came to the screen.

"If it is anywhere, it would have been here. Records indicate an instant entry for a new location. There is no record of build time or construction. It was simply not there one day, then the next a full structure. Its name and information were erased when the data was destroyed by the war. Such was the case with many servers. The explosions wiped much of the storage we have access to."

The screen zoomed in, to the area where the platform appeared, showing the location, and directions from Dome City. Nick pulled out his phone and snapped a picture of the whole screen. Since they had come to the city, the automated power stations had recharged all their devices. They were useless without towers, but could still be used for storage of data.

"What else can I help you with?" The voice returned.

"How can we use the gateway to get to Earth Prime?" Nick quickly asked.

"I am sorry, that information is not available at this time."

"What do you mean is not available?" Shabakaa said excitedly.

"The information has been blocked from your query." The voice added.

"Wait, blocked by whom?" Nick asked.

"That information is not available to you."

"Ok, when was it blocked?" Emma said moving to the edge of her seat.

"The block was added during the course of this query."

"Then it had to be someone who is currently in the city," Nick said making a face. "The individual who blocked this information, are they monitoring us right now?"

"Yes."

"The only one that I know of, who had control over city systems is G-25. Why would he be blocking our inquiries?"

"Maybe, he does not want you to leave. By doing this, he can keep you here." The computer's voice started to scramble as if it was being interfered with. The female voice's last words were, "It's here."

Chapter Sixteen: Friend or Foe

"We need to leave here now." The Professor said making his way to the door.

"Are we sure it is G-25, maybe there is another intelligence here. All these other systems are limited by the services they provide. So, G-25 did not lie about being the only one in that sense. But maybe there is another intelligence he did not know about. Something hidden to him." Nick tried to rationalize as they ran down the hall.

"Maybe even the worst thing of all." The Professor said with a wheezing sound. "What if the AI is not truly dead? What if, it was just reduced down to a smaller memory system, until enough recovery of the area, would allow its return."

"Slow down Professor, you are not that healed yet," Shabakaa said as he moved to the man's side and supported him.

"I will be fine my boy, but we have to get out of this city now."

"Agreed," Nick added. 'We also need to get G-25 to give me the restraining device, or this could turn much worse for us."

They made their way through the city, as lights appeared all along their way. It was as if someone was tracking their every move. As they ran, they saw movement from the corners of side streets and buildings. There was some sort of life. A life that was not there before. It had to be robotic in form.

The closer they got to the medical facility, the more it seemed the figures were closing in on them. Looking back as they ran, Shabakaa saw them coming. He let out a scream as he picked up his pace.

"Nick, they are right behind us." He said as he blasted past.

"Oh my god, how many are there?" Nick screamed as he tried to look back.

"More than I want to deal with," Shabakaa yelled as he reached the door of the building.

As the door opened, they raced in and barricaded it, before running to the room where they left G-25. The robots outside began to slam against the building as they reached their target. They were not as sophisticated as the AI of the past. It was as if they had limited operating capacity.

Nick flew through the door where he found G-25 holding the restraining device. The drone turned to him and held it up to the light. He was proud of what he accomplished. He was excited to help his new friends. He had no idea of what was happening outside the walls of the building.

"G-25, you said there was no other intelligent life in the city," Nick stated.

"Yes, none other than the workers that do not possess much more than operational programming. They are merely workers or assistants. They cannot function outside of the computer range. They were created to assist the humans before the AI took over." G-25 stopped speaking as he heard the rumble in the street of the robots slamming into the building. "What was that sound?"

"It is the robots being controlled by Artificial Intelligence. It seems something has been here all along. Hiding, growing, and waiting to make a comeback." Shabakaa said excitedly.

"How is it possible, I have never seen any signs of AI," G-25 said as he raised a screen, and zoomed in on the city street outside the building. "How is this happening? After all this time?"

"I don't know, but we have to leave this city now," Nick responded.

"Leave the Dome City? This is my home for all these years. I worked so hard to rebuild this place." The drone seemed confused.

"We don't have time to debate this. The longer we wait, the more of an advantage the AI has. All your hard work was only feeding the AI, and then it saw that we were here. It relaunched itself through the city's systems." Nick explained.

"I understand. I gave it life again. I rebuilt a city it could grow in. I made a miscalculation. I will correct it, but first I must save my friends. Nick, place this on your arm when you are ready and press the blue button. It will immediately restrain Anubis. I believe you will still have access to the nanites and their power source. Now, take the steps down just to the left of this door, there is a hidden exit there. You can make your way out and to the dome. It will open when you arrive." G-25's hologram face looked determined. He created this situation and he knew he had to correct it.

As the group ran down the steps, they saw the doorway G-25 told them about. Nick opened it slowly, onto an empty street. He looked back and forth, before motioning for the others to come behind him.

They left the building running as fast as they could. It was not a long distance to the dome wall, but they were determined to outrun the robots. Reaching the wall, they stopped at the edge, but nothing happened. Nick waved his hand in front of the doorway, but it remained closed.

"What the hell?" Nick screamed.

"The AI is holding it shut. It wants to give the robots time to reach us." Shabakaa said doubling over trying to breathe.

"It can't end like this. We can't go out this way." Emma grew angry and then saw G-25 approaching.

As the drone came closer, there was a full army of robots behind him. As he closed in on the group, so did the army. As G-25 approached the gate, he raised a hand and the doorway opened halfway.

"Go quickly, I do not know how long I can stop the AI from closing it." The drone shouted.

They filed through, one by one, until they all made it outside and G-25 followed. As he turned to look at the army, they slammed into the dome. Then G-25 raised a control device into the air. He took one last look, at the city he rebuilt as he pushed the bright red button. His final word, "Goodbye."

The city imploded from its center. From the outside, they saw the buildings fall one by one as the landscape cleared. G-25 made sure he had a backup plan in place. In this case, he set undetectable explosives throughout the power grid. He would not allow the AI to return a third time.

Chapter Seventeen: Escape to Nowhere

"Are we safe now?" Emma moaned as she fell to her knees.

"Yes, I am sure the destruction of Dome City, destroyed the network the Artificial Intelligence lived in," G-25 answered her.

"Not to mention all the other systems that serviced the city," Shabakaa said sarcastically.

"Yes, and those too. There was no other way. If I did not terminate all systems, then the AI would have jumped to a new location and started all over again." G-25 turned looking at all their faces one by one. "I take no joy in what I had to do. I worked hard to rebuild the city and bring its systems online. I did what was required, to stop the

AI from growing again, and taking over. You did not see what happened last time. You would not understand."

"No. You are right. We would not understand, since we were not here to experience the war." Nick paused. "Personally, I am glad we missed that experience."

"Me too," Emma added. "So, what now?"

"We have the information we retrieved from the archives," Nick responded.

"Not a lot of good there. What little was left, really did not say much." Shabakaa tried to push down his bad attitude.

"We did get a possible location for Atlantis." Nick lifted his phone into the air. "If it is still there, is the mystery."

G-25 looked at the map on the phone's screen and transferred it into his system. He raised his hologram hand into the air and formed a larger screen so that they could study it. Looking closely,

G-25 ran the image through his memory. He was sure he knew of that region.

"I have seen this place before." G-25 looked hard at the map, and then at the others. "The Badlands. I have heard stories of it. I went there once. It was not a place that was healthy for drones, or other electronic beings."

"What do you mean?" Emma asked.

"That part of the planet is prone to electrical storms and flares. They come out of nowhere. Before you know it, the charge in the air can be fatal. Systems that have a large metallic base, act like lightning rods for energy. One good zap, and a computer or even a living organism, could die quickly."

"And that is where we go next, right?" Emma began to laugh. "What will be thrown at us there?"

"Are you insinuating that the universe is against you?" G-25 tried to make sense of her comment.

"Which universe, we have been to many." She answered him. "I was joking. We have been through so much, and none of it makes sense. I guess I am just frustrated and would like to go back to my boring life on Earth Prime."

"Oh, my dear, your boring life will never be enough again." The Professor commented.

"What do you mean?"

"Pandora's Box has been opened and you are seeing all the things inside. Everyday life will drive you crazy now. You will desire the adventures we have been on. You will want more." He said smiling at her.

"Maybe you are right, but I do miss my friends and family so much."

The professor moved beside her and put his arm around her shoulder. "It's all going to work out eventually. Until it does, we are all your friends. Heck, we might just be a makeshift family."

"Yeah, I could do worse." She leaned into him and laughed. For a moment, everything was calm.

"G-25, have you figured out a direction, to take us to this supposed Atlantis?" Shabakaa said turning to the drone.

"Yes, I think I have a way to travel that will be acceptable to you humans."

"Then perhaps we should get moving. The sky and temperature are acceptable right now. Might just be a pleasant sightseeing trip." Shabakaa stood up and walked behind the drone. "You ever thought of a real name or anything?"

"You do not like my designation of G-25?"

"It's cool, I mean just a name like the rest of us. You look like us now. Hell, you look better than us." Shabakaa laughed. "Maybe we should call you Bob."

"That sounds kind of bland." G-25 spoke sounding unimpressed.

"No, I think it is perfect. Bob, it is."

Chapter Eighteen: On the Road to Atlantis

"We have been walking for three hours. How long is this trip?" Emma moaned.

"We have one hour to go," G-25 answered.

"G-25." Emma started to say before being interrupted.

"Bob!" Shabakaa added.

"Ok, Bob, this is what you thought would be an easy trip?"

"It would appear my version of acceptable to humans, and yours is slightly different."

"Your version?" Emma screamed.

"Ok children, calm down," Nick spoke up. "Before long we will be at our destination. Whether Atlantis is there or not. If it is not, then hopefully there will be a gateway there, right G-25 oh…Bob?"

"Yes, there will be a gateway and hopefully after all this time, it will be functional."

"Why would it not be functional?" Nick asked.

"The electrical activity may have destroyed its key systems. The only way we will know, is to get there and try to activate it." G-25 turned from the group who were becoming irritated by his honesty.

They walked for the last hour in almost total silence. The sounds of the animals and the birds around them, seem deafening. Exhaustion had set in, and no one was willing to pretend to be chipper. They all just dragged their feet, suffering through the pain in their bodies.

In the last twenty minutes, they approached a vision, none dared to hope was true. In the lower part of the ridge, was a body of water. Nick yelled out, as he began to run towards it. The others who had all become hot and tired, followed his example. They all forgot their worries, as they ran hard until the water splashed around them.

Emma threw water into the air and all around herself as she regained her strength. Even the Professor dove in and coated himself. It was the best-unexpected thing that could have happened. The water even piqued G-25's curiosity.

"Bob, come in with us," Shabakaa shouted.

"My friend, I may appear to be human, but the hologram only hides the electronic components. A good dip in the water, and you would no longer have Bob on your journey."

Their time in the water brought them all back from the edge of weakness. They gathered by the edge and took fruit from the trees. As they ate, the group began to speak again. The irritation with the planet and each other was ended. Friendship had returned.

"Bob, are you able to scan the area? Are there any signs of a civilization?" Shabakaa asked.

"Yes, there is something in the distance…that way. A large collection of buildings in a circular setting." G-24 answered.

"Are there any signs of life?" Nick asked.

"Inconclusive. Scans are being hampered by the electrical energy that is swirling through the area. I cannot get a good scan of any living things here except us."

"Then I guess we are going to have to be careful on the way in. At least we have a backup option from the gods." Nick said, raising the restraining bracelet into the air.

"I hope it does not come to that." The Professor said sighing.

"Me too Professor, but it is good to know, some good could come from having this inside me." Nick smiled as he turned to G-25. "Time to go see what we can see.

They walked around the water's edge and headed towards the direction of G-25's scan. No one knew what to expect or what might come their way. None of them were scared. They had come too far, to let the unknown scare them. Nick looked on in anticipation of seeing the fabled Atlantis.

As they grew closer, in the distance, the tall buildings of the platform came into view. Everything was in a circular pattern. Nick studied it as they grew closer. He saw the structure of what looked like a huge city, as well as, the base. He was sure this was at one time a spaceship. No wonder it disappeared so easily from Earth's history. It just went through the gateway, leaving a history of legends.

From a high tower in the city, a beacon lit as the sounds echoed inside the building. The group had been detected. "Do you have a visual yet?" The commander asked.

"Yes, there are three males, a woman, and an electronic signature. They are heading right for us." The science officer answered.

"Raise the cloaking device. I do not want them to know there are people in the city, until we are ready to initiate contact."

"Yes sir, understood. We are fully cloaked."

Chapter Nineteen: City of the Ancients

"It is amazing," Nick whispered as he stared at the architecture of the ancient city.

"Yes, but where are the people?" Emma asked as she scanned the stone streets.

"I have run a scan of the city within my limits." G-25 spoke up. "I think there is more here than meets the eye."

"What do you mean?" The Professor became curious.

"The structures are ancient but also maintained. If the city was deserted, then who has been doing their maintenance? Also, I am detecting electronic signatures all over the place. There are multiple power sources and electronics being used.

And, I detect heat sources, a lot of them. They are deceiving us. Probably a type of cloaking device. It might have worked on a mere human, but they did not anticipate a drone."

"Good job Bob!" Shabakaa belted out.

"Thank you, I think," G-25 replied.

"What do you do, when you come to the neighbor's house and ring the doorbell, as they turn out the lights?" The Professor asked.

"What does that even mean?" Emma was confused.

"Back on our earth, in the old days, it was a joke. If you did not want to talk to someone coming to your door, you just turn out the lights and pretend no one is at home. I do believe the Atlanteans are pretending to not be at home as well. Maybe we need to ring the bell a little louder."

"Yeah, I am not a fan of that one. Every time we do something like that, we find out the neighbors are big, scary, and violent." Emma joked.

"Well, if we do not ring, we will never know what we are dealing with. We might miss the opportunity to get home." Shabakaa added.

"Point taken. Now tell me how do we get their attention." Emma said as she looked around the street.

"Perhaps, that is something I can help with. G-25 spread his arms outward and began to levitate. As he moved upwards, his feet left the ground. In human hologram form, he looked like a god taking flight. As he climbed upward, he began to spin slowly and looked at all that surrounded him.

As he looked, he scanned for the right location where there were multiple heat signatures. "There you are, hiding grouped in a courtyard. Let's see how long you hide when you see this." Then, G-25 sent out a blinding pulse of EMP energy. Not enough radiation to harm the humans, but enough to let them know he was there.

As the pulse spread throughout the area, it dissipated as it hit the back sections of the city. The wave did what it was intended to do. The cloaking device began to fail, and with it, the scenery changed. G-25 floated back down to the stone-covered road below. The group watched as the ancient city came alive, with color and hidden people.

"That made a difference." The Professor said, please with the change.

"Yes, but are they going to see our entrance as hostile now?" Emma asked.

"Yes, I would assume so, since there is a small army headed our way." Shabakaa became worried. "I really do not want to be imprisoned, by a bunch of ancients. who G-25 pissed off."

"Stay calm and be reasonable, and we might just get out of this." The Professor said looking Shabakaa in the eyes.

"Why do you have to look at me like that? Like I am always the one to cause trouble?"

"Because…you usually are the one to cause trouble. You should really work on that." Emma said sarcastically.

"Maybe this is a discussion for another time. Right now, we need to be focused on them." Nick said separating the two.

From behind the group of soldiers, a man came forward. "I see we have uninvited guests."

"Hello, we meant no harm. Our drone was a little over enthusiastic to get your attention. He detected life and energy signs all around the city. He thought it was similar to ringing your doorbell, to see who was home." Nick tried to be diplomatic.

"Well, I am High Chancellor of Atlantis. I have no idea what a doorbell is, or how to ring it. What I do know is, that we do not take kindly to strangers, or those who send radiation through our city, to disturb our cloaking devices. We would have contacted you in our own time, when we felt it appropriate, and that you would not bring harm to our city. Since you did not allow us such luxury, I have but one alternative." He said as he turned to the small army behind him. "Guards, seize and detain them within the holding cells. And that one, the drone as they call it. See that he cannot set off any more destruction upon the city."

Chapter Twenty: The Creators

"How do we always bring out the worst in people?" Shabakaa whispered as they were led away.

"Probably a lack of good sense or thinking through what we do." Nick snapped at him.

"Oh no, you are not blaming me for this. I did not send Bob up in the air, and tell him to zap everything with radiation." Shabakaa became angry.

"Would both of you please shut up? You are not helping the situation. We should be focused on getting ourselves freed." Emma snapped.

"I am sure they will see the error of their ways. We just need to explain to them why we came here. This isn't what I hoped for, but at least we are in Atlantis." The Professor tried to restore order.

"Bob, why are you so quiet?" Shabakaa said looking at him with concern in his eyes.

"I have been scanning everything around us since the moment we arrived here. This city is an elaborate spaceship. There is no doubting that in its day, this would have been an impressive cruiser. Upon scanning its engines, I think I know why it has been here for so long." G-25 paused to avoid being overheard. "The engines are offline, and I believe cannot be restarted. At least not by the humans here. They either do not have the knowledge, or do not have the tools."

"How is that possible, they built this ship?" Nick questioned him.

"No Nick, we assume they built the ship. For all we know, it was built by some ancient alien race and left on Earth, where these people's ancestors found it. They probably used the tech on hand to teach themselves how to use the ship, eventually launch it through the gate, and who knows where else. Maybe, they accidentally launched it and ended up here, where they could not recreate what they did to cause the launch. Sound familiar?" G-25 slammed his point home.

'Ok, point taken. You would think after all this time, they would figure out how to fire this ship up." Nick could not understand why they stayed there.

"Maybe it is because you are right, and we have tried since the day we arrived, with no progress to speak of." A voice came from behind as the door to their cell was closed.

"Who are you?" Emma asked.

"I am Galen, and I am a scientist here in Atlantis. I am one of the ones who has been saddled with the task of bringing this ship back to life. So far, all the other scientists and I have been able to do is activate the city systems and defenses."

"Look, we did not come here to cause problems. We really do not want to be here or take anything from you. We are only seeking information, knowledge." Shabakaa insisted.

"I believe you. I have been watching. The High Chancellor is only being cautious, he will send an order to free you soon. I was surprised he let you get as close as he did. In the past, he hid the whole city from raiders. He values his people and is protective, but for good reason. After the past wars fought here, we have learned to hide in plain sight. We are a peaceful people; fighting is not our way. We are about technology, art, and betterment."

"Sounds like a wonderful place to be," Emma said as she smiled at the man.

"It would seem you are welcome to be here," Galen said as he received a message from a guard. "You are to come with me and have an audience with the High Chancellor."

As they walked, Nick told Galen of their experience in the gateway system and how they had traveled through the multiverse, trying to get home again. Galen was very sympathetic to their situation, being Atlantis has been stranded as well. They had gone from four stranded people to thousands in a few moments.

"Hello, I see you are in good spirits despite our awkward beginnings." The High Chancellor observed.

"Yes, we are well, and understand the need for what you did. If it were us, we would have done the same. I am Nick, and these are my friends Shabakaa, Emma, and Professor Newton."

"Hmmm." G-25 made a sound from behind Nick.

"And this is G-25, a recent addition to our group. He is from this planet."

"And where on this planet is he from?" The High Chancellor interrupted him.

"I am fully functional and can speak for myself." G-25 increased his volume. "I am from Dome City."

"It is as I feared. He came from the place of the Artificial Intelligence wars. They nearly destroyed this planet. If not for our cloaking device, we would have been discovered and drug into their insanity."

"With all due respect sir, the AI wars were a very long time ago. While they did devastate much of the planet, the source of the wars has been obliterated. As we left the Dome City, it was completely destroyed. I am the only survivor to my knowledge. I scanned the city for any survivors, and found no electronic signals, or any life at all for that matter."

"And how do we know you are not a carrier for the AI core program." The High Chancellor asked.

"I am more than willing to allow you to scan my systems. I have nothing to hide." G-25 stood his ground. "I am stuck here as much as any of the rest of you. I joined my group to seek a new life free of the AI programming. I seek freedom."

"Very well, but I will ask that you allow Galen to check your systems for any traces of AI."

"Agreed, please do so now, so we can put this behind us." G-25 grew tired of the line of interrogation.

As Galen ordered the equipment brought to him from his lab, G-25 allowed the process to begin. The probes scanned his programming to its core and the results were negative. Galen handed the tablet with the scan information to the High Chancellor. He seemed relieved at the results.

"Thank you, G-25, you must understand our safety is never jeopardized. It is protocol, we cannot allow anything to destroy the peaceful life we have created here." The man stopped for a moment and then looked at Nick. "I understand you came here seeking information. You need a way to get back to Earth Prime. I wish we had the means to help you, but we all came here the same way, by accidental travel. Yours might have been a lot less frightening as ours, when the whole city went into the gateway."

"This is frustrating to have the technology and not be able to use it." Nick sounded defeated.

"I know, but if you wish to stay here and use our city, you are welcome. Maybe together we can find a way home."

"What other choice do we have? We appreciate your offer and your kindness. Maybe together we can find a solution." Nick said sincerely.

"I wonder if the earth we left behind would still accept a city of travelers back amongst its people?" The High Chancellor turned and looked out over the city at his citizens peacefully going about their daily lives.

Chapter Twenty-One: Atlantis Reborn

In the days that followed, Nick and the Professor studied the systems in Atlantis. They were ancient technology, but still more advanced than modern people knew of. Nick made every reference to anything he had ever studied, as did the Professor. They moved slowly, but eventually, they made sense of the mechanics behind the city.

"I think we can reboot the systems with G-25's help," Nick yelled from underneath a platform, where he worked on an electronic panel.

"Agreed, with a little help, we should have this ship back online by nightfall." The Professor replied. "By the way, where is G-25?"

"For about three days now, they have been analyzing him. I guess they are really scared he has AI programming. Do you think they could be right?" Nick grew concerned.

"Anything is possible, but I just don't see how." The Professor stopped for a moment. "Why would he help us, if he was under AI control?"

"That's an easy one." Nick shook his head. "To gain his way into Atlantis. If G-25 did not know he had the subroutine, the AI could hide from him, until it was ready to grow. Oh god, just like we are trying to launch. If your home is destroyed, you look for a new one."

Nick jumped up and ran for the science division, where Galen was still scanning G-25. His fear took him over, as he realized once again, he had created a horrible situation. He led the Artificial Intelligence right where it wanted to go.

"Galen stop!" Nick screamed. "Move away from the drone."

"I don't understand. What has happened?" Galen had no idea what to think.

"There is a good chance G-25 has Artificial Intelligence in his system."

"Why do you think this?"

Nick took a deep breath as he tried to speak. "Before we left the Dome City, the AI released itself from one of the city's sub-routines. It began to spread through all the systems. We all left, but G-25 was there for a short time after we were gone. Then as he rejoined us, he detonated several explosions destroying the city. He said it was to make sure the AI was destroyed, but what if it had already uploaded into one of his subroutines?"

Galen moved backward from the drone. G-25 turned towards Nick, as his eyes began to glow red. A sinister look came over his artificial hologram face. Nick had never seen anything like it. He swallowed hard as he looked to Galen.

"Is he connected to any communications ports or electronics in the city"

"No, I made sure there was no way he could upload anything," Galen said as he stood shaking in fear.

"Are security protocols in place?" Nick asked.

"Yes. What would you like me to do with them?"

"Can you safely remove the AI programming from him?" Nick hoped there was a way. He did not believe in destroying any intelligent thing.

"I don't see how we can remove the AI without destroying his essential sub-routines. To get it out, we would have to wipe him clean. G-25 would no longer have memories or an operating system. He would be like a new unprogrammed drone." Galen said shaking his head.

"Is he contained in a shield?" Nick asked.

"Yes, he cannot get out of there."

"Can we move the shield, and him at the same time?" Nick ran many scenarios through his brain.

"In theory, yes. We could remove him from the city, but I do not know where to take him." Galen had never dealt with anything like this before, and it scared him to his core.

"If we can take him outside the city, we can then dispose of the AI. I do not want to risk it taking over the systems onboard Atlantis."

"I agree. I can levitate the platform he is on, and we can push it out of the city, in the direction you came in."

"Good. Let's do this now, we cannot risk him getting stronger or doing something we did not anticipate."

Galen raised the platform with the pushing of just a couple of buttons, and they began their journey towards the outer gates of the city. Galen used the universal announcement system to evacuate the streets they had to pass through. The citizens backed off in fear as they knew all too well what AI could do.

The Professor followed behind them as Emma and Shabakaa came forward. They watched in disbelief as the newest member of their team was carted away inside a containment shield. Emma hung her head, she liked G-25 and was getting used to having him around. She had a hard time understanding how this happened.

"Nick, be careful." She called out as they transported G-25 out into the area beyond the city.

Nick looked at the drone; he had just started to trust him. He felt betrayed and hurt. It seemed he could rely on little since they left home. The harder they tried to get back; the more obstacles appeared in their way.

He looked down to the bracelet that shined with a bright metallic glow in the sunlight. If he took it off, he knew he had the power to stop all this. In doing so, he would sacrifice G-25. He hung his head and tried to see all the options they had.

"Galen, are you sure that in wiping the Ai from him, we cannot retain a part of his original programming?"

"The AI is intertwined with his main operating systems now. To remove it, would damage him beyond repair. We could reload a new operating system, but what made him unique and intelligent would be gone. He would be an emotionless drone with no personal experiences or memory. He would be a computer."

"So, we destroy him?" Nick asked.

"It is all we can do."

Chapter Twenty-Two: Something Wicked This Way Comes

Nick ran his fingers over the bracelet. He looked to Galen with a saddened face. He knew he had no choice. What he had to do would not only save him and his friends, but all the citizens of Atlantis who were at risk. He slipped the bracelet off his wrist and put it into his back pocket.

"This is not easy Galen. I saw something in a movie back on my earth. It was about star travel. There was a horrible situation happening, where a main character was about to die. His friend sat on the outside of a protective glass and talked to him. The character knew he had to do something really brave to save everyone else on the ship from death.

So, he performed his task and was washed over in radiation.

When his friend, the captain of the ship asked him why he sacrificed himself, he said, "The needs of the many, out way the needs of the few, or the one." I always thought that was the bravest most unselfish way to die. I get it now, all those people in the city are worth losing one individual. They have to be protected."

"I understand, and that is a brave way of assessing a horrible scenario. I think I would like to see this movie one day." Galen turned towards G-25. "It is a shame to lose all that technology, but there is no other way."

As Galen moved further back, he waited for Nick's cue. Then he made sure the restraints did not allow G-25 to take flight. There was little more he could do, but watch Nick, as he moved just into the arch that stood beyond the city. It looked Ancient in nature but held no electronics.

Nick lowered his head and drew on the power deep within him. The nanites activated, as his eyes began to glow a bright blue. A grim expression covered his face as he felt the power flow through his body. Being a carrier for Anubis had its benefits.

As he raised a hand, G-25 ripped free of his restraints. He rose into the air; his expression and demeanor were so different. He appeared to be possessed, and in a way…he was. The drone they had come to know was no longer there. It made Nick's job a little easier.

As the drone spun around, it spoke for the first time. "You puny human, do you really think you are a match for me? I could kill you where you stand."

"You are wrong on two points. One, I am not a puny human, I am quite powerful. And two, you could not destroy me so easily. You see I am in a way a cyborg. I possess more power than you could ever imagine. You underestimate humans, we are capable of so much more than you understand. For a superintelligence, you are pretty closed-minded. I guess you really don't know everything."

As Nick finished his words, the drone climbed higher in the sky and prepared to strike him. As it unleashed a full-energy blast in Nick's direction, Galen ducked to the ground. Nick held up a hand, and deflected the energy aimed at him. Then, he smiled and said "My turn."

As Nick looked upwards, he unleashed the fire from within him. A bright blue filled the air all around the droid, as it found its target. The drone shook and vibrated as it tried to speak. "Perhaps, I did underestimate a human. Then again, you are no human. You are possessed with an intelligence just like me."

Nick looked hard at the drone. "Yes, I do have a technology inside me, but it is not AI and it can be controlled."

As Nick increased his hold on the drone, he began to tear it apart with energy pulses. Shooting deep within, the attack did what it was intended to do. The drone fell from the sky, landing in front of them. The glow of its red eyes began to diminish. Nick felt a sense of sadness for what had happened.

"You did what you had to do." Galen tried to comfort him.

"Yes, and if I believe that, I might just sleep at night. I should have never let my guard down. Every time I do…well you see the results. This time, we could have all ended up enslaved," Nick ran a hand through his hair as he turned away. He had beaten himself up enough for one day.

Galen scanned the drone for any energy signs, but there were none. The hologram that G-25 had created faded, and his original form showed through. Lying there on the ground was merely a hulk of metal and charred circuits. Nick had done his job well.

As Galen joined Nick, they walked back towards the city. Nick's eyes, returned to normal as he reached into his back pocket and retrieved the bracelet. Galen stared at the metallic ring, as his mind raced.

"Who gave you that thing?" Galen asked.

"G-25 constructed it for me in the city."

"Does it contain a memory system or any computerized systems?"

Nick looked down. "This is not a carrier, is it?"

Galen raised up a device he had placed in his coat pocket. He scanned the bracelet.   Then he smiled. "You are safe. No systems or storage detected."

"Hmm, maybe my luck is beginning to change," Nick said as he began to laugh.

Back near the archway, the drone lay on the ground. Silent and nonfunctional, except for an almost nonexistent beep that started out low, and then started to grow.

Chapter Twenty-Three: Back to Life

When they returned to the city, Nick felt the pain of regret. He did not like the idea of death, even if it did save the greater good. He rejoined the Professor just in time to reactivate the city's power core. It seemed there was some reason to rejoice.

"My boy, you look like you have the weight of the world on your shoulders. It is OK, to let it go. You only did what you thought you had to." The Professor's words were lost on Nick.

"I'll be fine. Probably even better when we get this ship underway."

"Good, because I have even better news. The ship only made the one jump through the gateway."

"So, what does that mean?" Nick was confused.

"It means, the ship's gate can just redial a return to its previous address." The Professor was excited to share the news.

"Can we see the address it came from?"

"No, only the gate has that stored information, and we cannot retrieve it. There are security devices in place to prevent that." The Professor understood Nick's question. They needed the address.

"When do we try the return?" Nick asked.

"The High Chancellor is to make the announcement in the next hour. Then we will start the process. We could be home tonight."

"I will hold my excitement until we actually get home," Nick said as he walked away.

Making his way to the edge of the city, he stood by the ancient structure. His mind roamed over their many stops on this journey. He really wished they were going home, but deep inside, he did not believe it. It all seemed too easy.

As Nick looked out into the area in front of him, his vision became cloudy. He threw his head back, and felt as if he were having a seizure. He blinked his eyes and tried to bring them back into focus. When he raised them again, there before him stood Anubis.

"I am sure you thought you had locked me away." Anubis snarled at him.

"No, I knew you were still in there, just watching and waiting." Nick stood his ground. "What do you want?"

"What I always wanted, control."

"Over me and my body?" Nick really did not have to ask.

"What else is there? We were matched perfectly. You are the perfect host for my implantation."

"Sorry, but I have other plans. With this bracelet, you have no power over me anymore.

You can just stay locked in the cage created for you." Nick said angrily.

"You never know, one day I might overpower that poorly designed piece of jewelry." Anubis' eyes began to glow.

"Maybe you will, but not today and maybe not in my lifetime. And maybe, just maybe I will find a way to rip you from my body. Then you would cease to exist without a host. Just think of that the next time you threaten me."

Nick turned to walk away, he felt good that he had defended himself and faced down a god. He was ready to return to his friends and get the ship underway. He walked back down the city street as he heard the sirens sound. Something was wrong.

Nick ran to the high overlook on one of the buildings. The ship's shields came online and raised to protect the city. As they were fully in place, Nick heard the blasting noises from the side. They were being fired upon.

The rest of the group joined Nick and looked out onto the army that was gathering just outside the perimeter. Pointing down Emma drew their attention to the leader of the attack. It was the leader Shabakaa, standing in all his shiny armored glory.

"How the hell did he get here?" Emma asked. "I thought he died."

"I would assume he escaped. I guess the older Nick only slowed him down. Then he followed us through the gateway somehow. Regardless, we have a jump to make. Professor, are the drives online?" Nick asked.

"Yes, we just have to tell the gate to redial and return."

"Then I suggest we do that before they break through the city's defenses."

With Nick's last words, a large blast hit the city. He turned to see an all too familiar form floating high above the army. G-25 was back online and at full power. He repeatedly took aim at the city as the army charged forward.

Nick and the others ran with the Professor as he headed to the gate room. The Professor powered up the crystals, as an announcement echoed through the city, telling everyone to find safety as the gateway opened.

The Professor looked at Nick as he pushed the activation crystal into place. The system powered up and a gateway opened. This one was larger than they had ever seen. It extended outwards and engulfed the city as Atlantis was pulled into the wormhole that extended into the network. As the city disappeared, one last large blast hit the outer shield.

Nick and the others were thrown to the floor as Atlantis started to shake violently while traveling forward. "Nick, this isn't right, we are out of control, this should not be happening. If this continues, the city will be destroyed."

"I know Professor, but there is no way to stop this process. It could cause more damage to leave the wormhole. We don't even know the gate addresses to go to. We have to ride this out. I just didn't plan to die today. Maybe someone else has other plans."

Chapter Twenty-Four: The Land of The Lost

As Atlantis bounced through the gateway, the violent movements, threw the citizens back and forth. Nick grabbed Emma as she was thrown to the edge of the upper balcony. She looked out at the side of the city as she screamed. There was no sky or sun, just flashing waves that filled the edges of the wormhole.

As they moved, the pulsing looked like lightning strikes on the city. Nick pulled her close and for a moment, she felt safe in his arms. She looked up and smiled at him. He was once again her protector. She wondered for how long.

"Nick, are we going to get through this." She asked. "This isn't the way it is supposed to be?"

"When we launched, G-25 hit us hard. With Shabakaa's army already attacking, I think they caused a rip in the wormhole. That is why we are bouncing." Nick tried to explain it all, still being uncertain of the facts himself.

"Why can't we just stop?"

"To do so, would mean we need an address that is close by, which we do not know of any. And we don't know how much stress that would put on the integrity of the ship. For all we know, with the ship's age and condition, it might rip apart or explode. We really have no choice but to ride it out."

"Well, we have been through a lot of other weird things lately, how can it get any worse?" Emma said as she began to laugh.

"We need to get to the others and make sure they are OK," Nick said taking her hand.

They made their way back inside as the building beneath their feet shook and rumbled. Emma remarked that it was like an earthquake she had experienced in California. Nick agreed, as he fell trying to stay upright. When they found Shabakaa, he was doubled over on the floor preparing to empty the contents of his stomach. The Professor was handling it much better, but he was still scared.

"Are you guys going to be OK?" Nick asked.

"Been better," Shabakaa said as he began to vomit to the side of the hallway.

"Professor, I am worried this city is not going to make it to the end of wherever we are going." Nick sounded scared.

"I agree, but what can we do? We can't abandon ship. We brought these people into this mess." The Professor felt the guilt of their attempt to help the Atlanteans.

"Just as well we don't even think about it. I don't even know, if we can gate out of a moving object, already in the wormhole." Nick said staring at the control board.

"Well, what a fine mess we are in now." The Professor moaned. "But not for long, I think the readout shows an exit ahead. Just don't know where."

The flying city blasted out of the end of the wormhole at what felt like lightspeed. The ship was designed to slow its descent after such events. This time it did not. The flying vessel traveled straight towards the planet's surface. They had no way of stopping their impending crash.

"Nick, dial the gate now. We are out of the wormhole, it should work." The Professor screamed.

Nick pulled the red crystal from his pocket and moved the others on the board to the only position he could remember. He was desperate for an address. Then the gateway powered up and opened a new wormhole.

The four stepped into the gateway as the ship began to crash down into the planet's ocean. Nick had no idea the splashdown was successful, or that the people all survived. He was ripped through space with the others on a trip towards the unknown.

As the wormhole opened at the destination, they flew out one by one rolling across the plant-covered ground. Emma sat up and immediately recognized her surroundings. She rolled her eyes as she raised her hands to her head.

"Are you freakin kidding me?" She yelled.

"I'd be careful with the yelling," Shabakaa whispered.

"Yeah, why?" She said sarcastically.

"Because there is a Tyrannosaurus rex just behind you in the tree line…and he looks hungry." Shabakaa jumped to his feet and began to move away.

As the T-rex began to move in their direction, Nick grabbed Emma's hand and they ran. Of all the places Nick could remember a gate address for, he wondered why the hell this one. He then convinced himself this was better than death.

Running through the trees, Shabakaa spotted a cave, higher on the hillside, in front of them. He sprinted towards it hoping no wild animals called it home. There was no time for second thoughts, they had to get inside.

As he grew closer, Shabakaa saw the carved steps to the side of the cave. Animals had not lived there, but perhaps primitive people had. The others joined him as he climbed feverishly up the side of the wall. He had once been into rock wall climbing and finally, it paid off.

Inside they ran to the back wall of the cave, where they found long tree trunks carved into pointed ramming posts. As the T-rex moved in, it stuck its head into the cave opening. Nick and Shabakaa grabbed a post and ran for the dinosaur's nose. They stabbed at it quickly and eventually rammed the post into its mouth, stabbing at it.

The dinosaur backed off as they retreated to the rear of the cave. Nick sat down and laughed at the situation they were in. He missed the days when he was bored in college. Then he remembered the creature that had helped them the last time they were there.

We have to find the forbidden city. We need Inak's lab if it still exists. He went to a different timeline, but since the dinosaurs still exist, then maybe what he left behind does too. We just have to stay alive long enough to get there."

The story continues in Nick Grainger Book 3 The Return Of Anubis.

Thanks for choosing this book, if you enjoyed it, please leave positive feedback.

Included at the end of this book, are the first chapters of G.W. Mullins' Best-Selling Series "The Convergence" Book Zero "Mass Destruction"

CONVERGENCE
BOOK ZERO

MASS DESTRUCTION

G.W. MULLINS

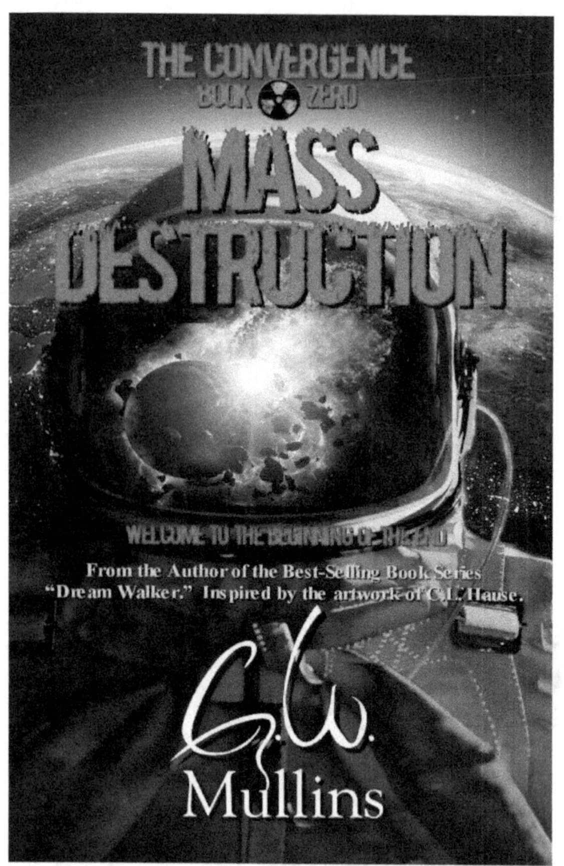

**The Convergence Book Zero
Mass Destruction
Is Available in
Hardback (978-1-958221-09-9),
Paperback (978-1-958221-08-2)
and various eBook formats worldwide.**

225

"I know not with what weapons World War III will be fought, but World War IV will be fought with sticks and stones."

Albert Einstein

"If we don't end war, war will end us."

H. G. Wells

THE
CONVERGENCE
BEGINS

Chapter 0 - The End Is Now

"Why do you look so scared, Comrade Patrick?" The Russian cosmonaut asked, as he laughed studying the other man's reflection in the glass of his console.

"I'm not scared, so much as I don't know how to react to the experience of floating free in space. I mean, this is the real thing." He replied.

"You chose to accept the position of captain of this spaceship they are building. What do they call it now? Discovery?"

"Who knows what it is called this week. All I know is, they are putting me through every training that is known to man." Patrick said, shaking his head as he turned to look out of the space station's window.

"I would not worry if they chose you, then they must be sure of your abilities. Besides, you may end up being one of the few who survive. Tensions are great, war is imminent. If your ship gets off the ground, you and the people living on it may be the last people of Earth."

"Wow, thanks…that was not too much pressure to put on me."

"Calm yourself, the spacewalk will commence in 15 minutes. You had better get suited up."

"Pavel, can I ask you something?" Patrick said staring into the man's face.

"Yes, what would you like to know?"

"If World War 3 does break out, would we still be friends?"

The Russian began to laugh, "What makes you think we are friends now? I am only kidding. We have known each other for some time. I do not trust very many people. You, I trust with my life. We would probably be friends no matter what."

Patrick turned and floated down the corridor. His stomach turned at the thought of what was before him. He doubted himself, and the role he would lead in saving mankind. If the war did not kill humanity, the state of the environment was about to.

The environmental crisis that was spreading across the earth was unrepairable. The planet would be uninhabitable in less than five years. The governments knew it was coming for decades, yet they did nothing until it was too late. Now, instead of doing whatever they could to save lives, they were on the verge of nuclear war.

A group of scientists came together and formed the concept of the ship Discovery. It would serve as a record of human life, and a way to preserve a small group of humans. The ship would feature the latest in space pod living, and feature holographic technology, that would create a world that looked just as the earth did, for the regions the groups of people would be taken from. In a sense, they would never know they had been relocated to the ship. There could be no mass hysteria if the people were unaware, they even left their homes.

The real challenge was, to get Patrick trained and the ship completed before the first nuke was launched. The estimated departure was to come in two weeks. There was no time for error or unsureness of the new ship's captain. Patrick knew this, as he began to pull on his space suit. Breathing deeply, he was no amateur and he knew it. Lives depended on him.

As the door opened into deep space, Patrick stared out in awe. It was everything he had hoped it to be. His fears were behind him, as a smile crossed his face. He checked his readings one last time as he floated in the doorway.

"Well, are you going to float there all day, or are you going out?" Pavel teased him.

"I am going out. Oh, and Pavel, don't let anything happen while I am out there." Patrick joked.

"What could happen? There is nothing going on here except space. Maybe the settlement on the moon's surface might drift past as you are finally going out the door."

"I cannot believe we finally settled the moon," Patrick said looking towards the lights on the surface. "Man, that is beautiful."

As Patrick finished his last words, he floated outwards away from the station's doorway. He breathed deeply, as he moved around and saw the earth below him. He didn't know what to think, being so far away looking in. He finally found his strength and courage.

Patrick turned around and looked back to the moon. The structures were very clear to him from his distance. They looked like a small city, like you would find in some quiet corners of the earth. Except, there were no quiet corners anymore. The days of quiet were gone years ago. They went with the plague that came after Covid. Too many lives were lost, too many mistakes were made. No one knew of the side effects the cure would have.

As Patrick floated deep in his thoughts, a bright light shot in his direction. He struggled to see what was going on. "Pavel, what was that?" He waited, but there was nothing except silence. Then a second blast, and he knew what was happening.

As the moon rattled, and then debris shot into space, a huge chunk of rock flew at Patrick. He pulled at his harness feverishly, quickly moving out of the way. Then as his body drifted in space, he turned and saw the destruction. The moon was blasted in two, separated almost down the center. The lights on the surface came from nuclear explosions. He was sure of that. "Pavel, do you hear me?"

"Yes, Comrade, it was nuclear in nature. Word is spreading across all channels. There have been explosions back home as well. You are ordered to come back to the station. We are at war. It has begun…the end of life as we know it is upon us."

Chapter 1 – Six Months Ago

"Hostilities are growing between the United States and Russia. While the United Nations is struggling to bring some resolution, several other countries have entered the hostilities, many of which are communist. The fear of war is looming."

The sound from the monitor speakers echoed throughout the former NASA space center. The massive workforce stopped in unison, as they looked towards the screens which lined the massive halls. In that moment, there was no other sound, but the news anchor's voice.

Many bowed their heads in silent prayer, for a solution to the inevitable event that was coming fast upon them. Others turned back to their work. They knew if they did not finish as scheduled, there would be no reason to build the massive metal structure, that rested between the buildings in front of them.

Patrick walked the hall, making his way to the command center. As he looked out of the window, at the puzzle pieces before him, he could see the ship taking shape. He shook his head, thinking this ship was like something out of an old space movie. If it worked, it would be spectacular.

The ship was broken into several pod cities, which sat side by side on the outer platform. All of which would be connected by a main central ship. The ship even had its agricultural pod, to constantly produce food and oxygen. Patrick smiled, as he realized he would captain this massive starship.

His joy turned, as Patrick faced the reality, that only a select group of people would be chosen to go into space. He found it cruel that the whole process of saving humankind would be cloaked in deceit. Those left behind would certainly die as the global ecosystem disintegrated, from pollution or radiation.

He felt a lump in his throat, as he faced the reality, that family and friends would not survive. Today, that would not be his greatest concern. Discovery had to be finished on time. So far, that seemed like an attainable goal.

"It's beautiful, isn't it?" A female voice came from behind him.

"Yes, it is. I just never thought it would come to this." He answered.

"I am Major Carter. I am supervising the pod's construction and testing all holographic installations in the cities within."

"Hello, I am Alexander Patrick. I am for lack of a better term, the captain."

"I am aware. Don't let it overwhelm you. This is a great honor to be chosen to head this ship. You are going to save a lot of lives."

"Yeah, and they won't even know it. They will go to bed one night, and then wake up the next morning, not even knowing they are on a spaceship transplanted into a holographic world, not of their choosing." Patrick grumbled.

"It is necessary. If word got out that we were selecting individuals to go on this ship, or even that the ship existed, we would be bombarded with people trying to force their way onboard. We can barely handle the size of the group we are taking. There just is no fair way to go about this." She sighed knowing she was never going to make herself believe it, let alone another person.

"Will we make the deadline?" He asked.

"Yes, I believe we will, as long as no one sets off a nuke. Seems like many countries have their fingers ready to push the launch buttons."

"Carter, you are very high up in the government. So, you would know…what are the chances of anyone surviving if multiple warheads are launched?"

"Life on earth as we know it, would be gone. There are safer locations and chances some people would find safety, but radiation would wash over the planet. Whatever would still exist, would be changed, and civilization would crumble. All major cities would soon be uninhabitable. Ever watch a zombie movie?"

Patrick turned back to the window and swallowed hard. He knew she was right. Then, he felt guilty, he was going to survive the possible holocaust, while millions died. He thought hard and then forced the unsettled feeling to the bottom of his stomach. He had to be strong. People would be depending on him.

He turned back and looked at Carter. "What about you?"

"What about me?" She asked

"What will happen to you?"

"I will be going with you. I have been granted passage on the ship. You will need someone to head engineering, and I am as qualified as anyone." She said smiling.

"Good, I am happy you will be safe."

"None of us will be safe, until this ship breaks free from the atmosphere, and gets out of attack range."

"You think they would shoot us down? That is crazy." He said in anger.

"No, that is real life, and in a war, you take down the one with the advantage. They don't want to see us succeed, while they stay behind to die. In a rational world, I would like to think everyone would like us to make it into space. Then…there is nothing ration about nuclear war."

"I guess, we work to make this happen. No matter how we have to do it."

"I hear they have a series of training sessions for you. Including a spacewalk. I can only imagine what that will be like."

Patrick looked upwards, staring into the sky. He had never been outside the Earth's atmosphere. He craved the experience, but still, he had an element of fear inside him. He wondered if it was all too much too soon.

Carter walked over and placed her hand on his shoulder. He turned to her and smiled. He knew she was trying to comfort him, but he had his demons to deal with. She smiled back at him as they both turned to the window and looked upwards. Their future was right in front of them.

Chapter 2 – The Ship of The Future

The morning news brought the world one step closer to the brink. North Korea, once again went against threats from the world and tested another nuclear warhead. The explosion came with a warning to the United States. Any interference would result in retaliation.

President Jones, stood his ground, as he defended the country and his pride. Even he knew, there was no winning in this war. We were doomed, no matter who fired first. He could only hope to hold out until Discovery was launched.

The weeks flew past, as Patrick saw his spacewalk approaching. The ship began to take shape, as the massive dome cities were attached to the main body. In the days after, Patrick walked the ship and took in all he would be captain of. He had grown up watching Star Trek, and he tried to think of this as his enterprise. It was a far cry from being that advanced, but it was so much more than he expected.

As he entered the first dome city, the hologram, automatically engaged. An electric grid formed all around him, and as he watched, the shapes of metal walls and glass windows disappeared. Where there were once smooth metallic shapes, there were now glowing lines that converged together taking form.

On the massive floor before him, the shapes of buildings and grassy fields emerged. Patrick stood back in awe of the holograms. He had never seen anything like it before. In a matter of seconds, a small country town was erected.

Patrick walked in the field of grass, that swayed in the breeze. He kneeled and ran his hand through the blades. It felt real. He knew in his mind it was a projected material, but to his sense of touch, it was still real.

He fell back onto the ground. Laughing out loud, he could not contain himself. It was all real to him, from the plants to the sound of birds in the trees. Even the feeling of the breeze caressed his cheek. He couldn't tell the difference.

Then, he thought of those who would be transplanted there. They would not know either. They would just think, they were home. It was still a lie, but they would know no difference. At least he thought, they would still be alive.

"I see you have come to know Carson Corners."

Patrick flipped around to see Carter heading his way. "Yes, this is so much more than I expected. It feels like I am on earth. I did not know things like this were possible."

"It wasn't, until very recently, and then we kept it a secret since it has so many military applications."

"Something so wonderful, that could be used for so many good things, has to be hidden from those who would abuse it." Patrick reached out and touched the grass, trying to understand why people were abused so much in the world.

"Welcome to the real world," Carter said walking away.

"Well, almost. The world we soon would have lived in."

"This one has its advantages. Like health care, and controlled weather. You can even summon help if you know what to ask for. Watch this…emergency care needed, medical."

As she finished speaking, directly in front of them, a distortion in the holographic field formed. The image of a man took shape, as a brilliant light swirled in place.

"I am Holo-tech Medical Assistant 1, please state your emergency." The figure stood before them, as the light he emitted flicked and fizzled.

"Hmm, that is strange, he is having trouble taking form. I'll have to look into that, it should not be happening. Still, it is new, and there is always some issue to fix." Carter said staring at the hologram.

"PPPPPlease state your emergency." The hologram asked.

"There is no emergency. This is only a test. One that is failing miserably. Disengage Medical Assistant. This will have to be looked into"

As Carter spoke, the hologram disappeared into the electrical grid. Patrick watched in disbelief of the technology, as everything returned to normal. The hologram system was intelligent and could add to itself at will.

"Carter, if the people living here are not supposed to know about the hologram, how are you going to use the medical assistant?"

"Easy, he will appear, as if in a hospital setting or as a doctor making a house call. He can change himself to fit any situation, just like the holographic grid can adapt to fit the need. We can add terrain, add buildings, or add roads and land as a person travels. In most cases the hologram moves, the person does not."

"This will take some getting used to. All I ever saw a hologram do was perform in concert." Patrick said knowing he was out of his ballpark.

"Oh, you saw those disgusting holographic pop stars? They were awful, I am glad they have been phased out. Still, if we didn't start there, we would not have gotten to this point. Now, imagine a complete town or city like this in each pod, fully functional, programmed to expand and create new things as needed."

"I would say that is a lot of room for error." He laughed.

"Unfortunately, and that is why we are testing and perfecting before Discovery gets off the ground. In space, there is nowhere to find out, we made a mistake."

"At least, you will be there to help fix what may go wrong."

"I would rather get it right before liftoff."

As the two walked forward, the land before them, extended and continued in any direction they chose to go. The hologram seemed to work in every way, except where creating people was concerned. That seemed like the least of their problems.

About the Author

Thanks for choosing this book, if you enjoyed it, please leave positive feedback.

G.W. Mullins is an Author, Photographer, and Entrepreneur of Native American / Cherokee descent. He has been a published author for over 14 years. His writing has focused on the paranormal and Native American studies.

Mullins has released several books on the history/stories/fables of the Native American Indians. Among his books are the extremely successful "Star People, Sky Gods and Other Tales of the Native American Indians," "Story Teller An Anthology Of Folklore From The Native American Indians," "The Native American Story Book - Stories Of The American Indians For Children Volumes 1-5," "The Native American Cookbook," and "Walking With Spirits Native American Myths, Legends, And Folklore Volumes 1 Thru 6."

He has released the complete series of his Sci/fi Fantasy books "From The Dead Of Night," including the Best-Selling titles – "Daniel Is Waiting" and "Daniel Returns." His most recent work includes the series "Rise Of The Snow Queen" featuring Book One "The Polar Bear King", Book Two "War Of The Witches", and Book Three "The Story of Gerda And Kai."

Mullins' latest releases include two young adult fantasy series, "Rise of the Darklighter" Book One "Dark Awakening," Book Two "Night Of The Demon" and the "Dream Walker" Book Series featuring "Enter the Sandman" and "Wide Awake In Dream Land." Among his other releases are "The Legend Of White Bear (Extended edition)" a Native American paranormal shapeshifting story, "Messages from The Other Side" (a nonfiction book about communication with the dead), and the currently releasing "The Convergence" (a post-apocalyptic book multi-series event).

WELCOME TO THE END OF LIFE AS WE KNOW IT
THE FINAL DESTRUCTION
BEGINS NOW
THE CONVERGENCE
The Convergence
Book 0
Mass Destruction
In Stores Now
The Convergence
Book 1
Armageddan
In Stores 5/2023

For further information, on his writing, visit G.W. Mullins' website at
http://gwmullins.wix.com/books.

Nick Grainger And The Search For Atlantis

Also Available From G.W. Mullins

Haunted America

Night Of The Walkers

The Convergence Book Zero Mass Destruction

The Convergence Book One Armageddon

Rise of the Darklighter Book One Dark Awakening

Rise of the Darklighter Book Two Night Of The
Demon

Rise Of The Snow Queen Book Four The Frozen
Heart

Rise Of The Snow Queen Book Three The Story Of
Gerda And Kai

Rise Of The Snow Queen Book Two The War Of
The Witches

Rise Of The Snow Queen Book One The Polar Bear
King

Daniel Awakens A Ghost Story Begins– From The Dead Of Night Prequel

Daniel Is Waiting A Ghost Story – From The Dead Of Night Book One

Daniel Returns A Ghost Story - From The Dead Of Night Book Two

Daniel's Fate A Ghost Story Ends - From The Dead Of Night Book Four

Dream Walker Book Two Wide Awake In Dream Land

Dream Walker Book One Enter The Sand Man

Nick Grainger Book One The Curse Of Cleopatra

The Legend Of White Bear (Extended Edition)

Messages From The Other Side Stories of the Dead, Their Communication, and Unfinished Business

Vengeance – A Paranormal Mystery

Nick Grainger And The Search For Atlantis

Mysteries Of The Unseen World – Ghost, Hauntings and The Unexplained

Haunted America Stories Of Ghost, Hauntings And The Unexplained

Timeless – A Paranormal Romance Murder Mystery

Star People, Sky Gods, And Other Tales Of The Native American Indians

More Star People, Sky Gods, And Other Paranormal Tales Of The Native American Indians

Aliens, Gods, and other Paranormal Native American Tales

Buffalo Tales Of The Native American Indians

Coyote Tales Of The Native American Indians

Bear Tales Of The Native American Indians

Lost Tales Of The Native American Indians Vol 1

Lost Tales Of The Native American Indians Vol 2

Walking With Spirits Native American Myths,
Legends, And Folklore Volumes One Thru Six

The Native American Cookbook

Native American Cooking - An Indian Cookbook
With Legends And Folklore

The Native American Story Book - Stories Of The
American Indians For Children
Volumes One Thru Five

The Best Native American Stories For Children
Cherokee A Collection of American Indian
Legends, Stories And Fables

Creation Myths - Tales Of The Native American
Indians
Strange Tales Of The Native American Indians

Spirit Quest - Stories Of The Native American
Indians

Animal Tales Of The Native American Indians

Nick Grainger And The Search For Atlantis

Medicine Man - Shamanism, Natural Healing, Remedies And Stories Of The Native American Indians

Native American Legends: Stories Of The Hopi Indians Volumes One and Two

Totem Animals Of The Native Americans

The Best Native American Myths, Legends And Folklore Volumes One Thru Three

Ghosts, Spirits And The Afterlife In Native American Indian Mythology And Folklore

War Song: Tales Of The Native American Indians

For books available from G.W. Mullins in
Hardback, Paperback and eBook

Visit: https://gwmullins.wixsite.com/books

Or scan the QR Code below

Links to G.W. Mullins pages are on Linktree
https://linktr.ee/gw.mullins

From the Author of the Best-Selling Novel Daniel Is Waiting
Rise of the Snow Queen
Book 1
Sometimes Fairy Tales Don't Have Happy Endings
The Polar Bear King
G.W. Mullins